DIPLOMAT, WITHOUT PORTFOLIO

Bedros Anserian

Copyright © 2024 Bedros Anserian
All rights reserved
First Edition

NEWMAN SPRINGS PUBLISHING
320 Broad Street
Red Bank, NJ 07701

First originally published by Newman Springs Publishing 2024

ISBN 979-8-88763-164-6 (Paperback)
ISBN 979-8-89308-749-9 (Hardcocer)
ISBN 979-8-88763-165-3 (Digital)

Printed in the United States of America

Dedication to my wife Marianne Anserian and two children
Hagop Anserian and Alexandra-Klavdia Anserian

PREFACE
BEDROS ANSERIAN—FAMILY BIOGRAPHY

Since childhood, I was raised with close family members around me or in our house. As a member of an Armenian family, traditions and respect toward the elderly were part of my life. I remember very well that every time I met my grandma, I was supposed to kiss her hand and then proceed to talk. I would talk to my grandma in Armenian, and she would respond in Turkish. She was not permitted to talk in Armenian in Aintab, Turkey, where she was forcibly deported, along with my grandfather and my father for nine months in her lap. I was supposed to speak very politely while asking my questions. I was supposed to be discreet and talk with a low voice. Since I bore my grandfather's name, whom I never met, and I was also the first male grandchild of the family, I was somehow given more attention and affection.

Once I finished my elementary school and was admitted to high school, I had more flexibility to speak with my parents and family members. By now, I was capable of communicating with my grandmother in Turkish and was even able to do her shopping requests.

We were three brothers and one sister in the family. I was the oldest son, and my sister, the youngest. Three brothers shared a big room, and each one of us had a special corner in the room with various decorations and gadgets.

My sister and I attended Armenian high schools, but my two younger brothers attended local public high schools since they were brilliant in the Arabic language.

Our relationship was perfect with one another and with our parents. Father worked at two locations, employed with the local government, and was a blacksmith on his own. He had to cope with our expenses.

Since school was half day on Wednesdays and Saturdays, I used to carry his lunch to his second workplace, where he prepared gas tanks and accessory compartments for trucks and buses. The chief mechanics of the workplace were my two younger uncles, Georges and Abraham, and the youngest uncle, Vartan, was an employee, with whom we had a fantastic relationship relating to sports and mechanical backgrounds. With great interest and enthusiasm, I watched the operation of each machine in the workplace while waiting for my father to finish his lunch. He used to tell us that he wanted to get his revenge by sending us to high school and university. He had been pulled out of his school when he was only nine years old and joined his father to help him secure income for their family.

Maybe that was the reason my younger brother graduated as a mechanical engineer and his grandchildren as a system engineer and business computing.

We were a happy family altogether; frequently, we got together. Picnics were part of the family activities, and our respect and behavior were always highly appreciated by all our family members. This continued and stamped our characters and anchored our children too.

In my high school days, I used all my qualifications in sports and music, thus impressing my classmates as a good basketball and guitar player. We had our own school band, and we played some of the Beatles' songs. Also, being a basketball player, I was a standby player in our high school team.

I was considered an above-average student in the school for my good grades and polite attitude. I was chosen the class leader for the two last years of my high school years. The school attendant, Mr. Donabedian, used to change that with my other classmates every three months.

I was acting as a leader in my class, and with various activities, I was given the chief title of all my classmates.

We had no chance to celebrate our graduation ceremony at the end of my high school year. Due to the Israeli-Arab war of 1967, we were supposed to stay indoors and only circulate during the necessary class periods. Our graduation ceremony was a secret indoor ceremony attended by only the principal and the teachers without our parents.

I was lucky to be accepted to the American University of Beirut; I studied business administration. Since the family's financial situation was not adequate, I tried to obtain the required minimum credits only to cope with the necessary expenses. At the end, after so many years, I completed my studies and was awarded my diploma.

I worked as a bookkeeper and then as an assistant accountant at a Nazarian/Markarian manufacturing company. I then applied to various embassies to get a better job and to secure more income for myself.

I was interviewed by the American embassy in Beirut, and after six to seven months of background checks, I was hired to work as a visa clerk. Within one year's time, I was given the supervisory job of the consular section. I studied the visa manuals and was given the privilege of studying the US Department of State's correspondence course and successfully completed the courses and obtained my certificates.

I was chosen as one of the first foreign citizens to attend the Foreign Service Institute for the Professional Consular Training Program in Washington, DC, and I received the corresponding certificates.

By this time, I was well known to the Lebanese community, especially in the Armenian communities in Lebanon and Syria. As a supervisor of the consular section, I attended every meeting that the chief of the consular section was attending with the minister of foreign affairs and the chief of Internal Security Forces in Lebanon. I was the liaison employee between the embassy and these two government representative offices.

After three years of my employment with the American embassy, I met my dream girl, Marianne H. Tatevossian, and got married, after being engaged to her for a year. Our marriage ceremony was postponed by a week due to the start of the civil war in Lebanon. I was not able to leave the house due to the bombing of our residential area. Christian militants suggested taking me to the church by military vehicle, but I preferred to postpone it so that my family members and the embassy staff would also have the chance to attend. And it happened—we got married a week after the scheduled date; it was July 6, 1975.

We had our own house in the same building where my parents lived, and life seemed very normal, until the civil war deteriorated. The frequent bombings were daily incidents, and I was not able to cross the confrontation line of the two sections (Christian and Muslim or East and West) of Beirut. The embassy's location was in the west part of the city.

I was given an embassy apartment, and I lived there for a time. I was able to cross the home side every weekend if the security situation permitted to do so. I celebrated my first wedding anniversary without my wife. I was in the west side, and my wife was in the east side; we congratulated each other over the phone.

Life was difficult and dangerous. With every precaution, I tried to survive and secure an income for my new family.

During this period, the consular work was a priority. Everybody tried to survive and secure visas in that disturbed situation, and we had hundreds in front of the consulate applying for their visas. We hired additional employees, and I had to supervise a group of twelve employees.

This did not last long, and the civil war entered its "hottest" period, and after the assassination of the American ambassador Francis Melloy, I was asked to wrap up the consular files and keep them safe.

Diplomat, Without Portfolio

A top secret decision was made, and I was asked to prepare myself for an evacuation in October 1976. After all the preparations, I was evacuated by a US warship, along with my colleague officers, to Athens, Greece. Luckily my wife was with me at that time, and she accompanied me as a dependent.

While working in Athens, I mingled with the personnel of the American embassy in Athens and the regional immigration office. I obtained a good experience in handling immigrant and visitor visa rules and regulations.

After the departure of our Beirut-assigned officers from Athens, I was alone with one Lebanese employee and handled all the Beirut files and cases for a continuous one-year period.

Athens gave me the opportunity to learn more regarding visa rules and the different ways of handling them and, of course, the local Greek language too.

Beirut, by this time, had a truce treaty between warlords and the Christian-Muslim representatives and the Arab Deterrent Force, so we were asked to return to Beirut.

We reestablished the consulate in Beirut and rehired our employees and began to resume normal consular operations in the American embassy in Beirut.

They were difficult days, and we still had the main confrontation line and crossing from one side to the other.

For my family and me, it was a good start upon our return from Athens. My wife gave birth to our first child, Hagop, in May 1977. And we were happy and busy with reestablishing the whole situation in our family, as well as with our child.

Additional responsibilities and family affairs kept me around my family and my parents and my in-laws. Although we were a united and tight family, I was sharing with my wife all kinds of responsibilities at this time—shopping, visiting pediatrics offices, and then enjoying Hagop's presence and administering to his various schedules.

Our parents on both sides were very helpful; they would take care of Hagop while we were out of the home. And these were positive moments for me and my wife while enjoying the calm period of the truce. We were dividing our babysitting duties between my parents and my in-laws—the in-laws in the morning, and in the evening, my parents. I and my wife easily reported to our daily duties and, in case of any night visits to friends, were secured with babysitting issues.

We were blessed that the relationship between my parents and in-laws were calm and amicable and that we had no misunderstandings of any kind or any frictions in both families, and this encouraged us to develop a healthy and kind relationship with family members and to concentrate on the development of our child.

The calm situation did not last long; the presence of Syrian forces in Lebanon created various kinds of problems and panic in all families—in the Christian side especially, where our house was located.

Once again, crossing between the East and the West became dangerous, and daily crossing was even worse after certain hours of the day. Seeing the difficulty of the crossings and reporting to duty on time, the embassy administration offered empty apartments that belonged or were rented by the embassy. I was sharing with another colleague in one of these apartments around the embassy premises. In this situation, my wife and my child joined me in the west (Muslim) side of the city, and we lived a long period of time in West Beirut.

We used to visit my parents and in-laws on weekends and report to duty regularly. Marianne got permission from her father to stay with my son rather than join her father in their rug-selling shop, where she was helping her father in rug repairs, in East Beirut.

We had our own friends on both sides, and on occasions, we had get-togethers and, sometimes, visits to secure locations on Mount Lebanon and were surviving with a hope of "Tomorrow will be a better and safer day."

The family faced a tragedy in this period when, within forty days, we lost my father-in-law and mother-in-law. Marianne, eight months pregnant, was obliged to run her father's business and, at the same time, tried to stay safe on the east side—near my parents and near the hospital—ready for delivery. The birth of my daughter, Alexandra-Klavdia, in December 1981 changed the whole mood of the family. It was a joyous and happy gathering. We welcomed Marianne and my daughter home, and I stayed for almost fifteen days at home, helping my wife and the family.

Our expectations didn't last long, and we faced real dangerous periods too. I was obliged to leave the family this time in our home (East—Christian side) and report to duty in West Beirut, the Muslim side. It was a very dangerous crossing.

I was beaten and kidnapped by Syrian soldiers for no reason, while crossing to West Beirut, for a couple of hours in May 1982, and I was lucky to get my release through an Armenian friend and get back to my old Mercedes after a while. I stayed at home a couple of days, and then after my recuperation, I resumed my duty. Due to various roadblocks by militias, I faced insults and interrogations every time I crossed to the side. The situation had nothing to do with being Christian or Muslim; even our West Beirut friends were suffering this dilemma. I was lucky that one of our employees—motor pool supervisor Sarkis, a gray-haired middle-aged man—accompanied me in driving my car every day back and forth to West Beirut.

Bedros Anserian

West Beirut became a real dangerous location, and the employees faced various harassments too. As a member of Embassy Employees Association, I and a group of East Beirut resident employees initiated a request to the embassy administration to secure the East Beirut employees with a bulletproof van to cross altogether the confrontation line, which was a busy operation location for the snipers from both sides of the city. The request was approved, and we were supplied with an armored van. Unfortunately, this didn't last long, and after a while, I requested they furnish us with dormitories in the upper floors of the seven-floor embassy premises. Within a few weeks, we had our dormitories, and we used to work and sleep in the same building for almost six to seven months.

Due to Israel's invasion of Beirut in the summer of 1982, the embassy shut its doors, and we went home without knowing about our future.

Staying at home without work and without knowing about our future was confusing, and it was an unexpected dark period. Although I had all kinds of encouragement by my wife, my parents, and family members, I felt guilty of not having work. After almost three weeks, I was asked to join one of my colleagues, Officer John, to help him in locating US citizens in East Beirut. We planned, and for a while, the back of one of our embassy cars was our office desk. We were typing our letters in the back of the car. We worked together, and in a short period of time and with my connections and contacts, I convinced the mayor of the city of Jounieh to establish a temporary consulate in Jounieh City Hall. My request was accepted, and we began to work from the city hall, supplying our US citizens with cover letters to secure their exit from Port Jounieh. Jounieh was a military port and had no permission, and it was not supposed to operate as a civil transportation port.

We managed to get all the permissions to link Port Jounieh with Larnaka Port, Cyprus—this was a secure passage for our citizens out of Beirut.

During this period, the family members were happy that my work office was located in a safer location rather than in a dangerous place—although it was a hectic job working in an environment with various kinds of people who were desperately attacking you and requesting various kinds of services, visas, etc., which we had no means to supply.

The temporary consular section was an office just to supply directions rather than services. Little by little, it became an operative temporary consular section and issued very high emergency visitor visas and recommendation letters only to US citizens.

This didn't last too long after the assassination of President Bashir Gemayel. We got orders to prepare an evacuation for the remaining US citizens from Port Jounieh. It was a long one-day procedure, and I was involved as a liaison person between the ambassador's residence and Jounieh City Hall. After the peaceful evacuation, we continued to work in Jounieh City Hall for a couple of weeks more; and after the withdrawal of the Israeli Army from Southern Lebanon, we resumed our duty in the embassy premises in West Beirut.

Sarkis was my right-hand man in Jounieh, and he helped us a lot. After we resumed our duty in West Beirut, we continued to cross the confrontation line together. He used to come early in the morning and had his morning coffee at my home, and then we continued our journey toward West Beirut to the embassy.

Even my parents were very close with Sarkis; they used to invite him to their condo located on the second floor of the same building where I was residing to chat about the "daily news" and, sometimes, drink the morning coffee together. This lasted for almost six months.

Bedros Anserian

It became a routine to cross the confrontation line in the early morning before the traffic jam and be in the office for Lebanese breakfast—manousheh (bread with thyme).

*****

It was Sunday; I and my wife were invited to a friend's wedding and reception party. We came back home in the early hours of the morning, and I was tired. I left all my clothing on the hanger in the bedroom and woke up with difficulty. Marianne prepared my coffee, and after wearing the same suit that I wore to the wedding and after getting the goodbye kiss from Marianne, I jumped in my car as I was running late to the office. Sarkis was on vacation, so I was supposed to drive the car very cautiously without ignoring the eye contact of the militias while arriving at the various roadblocks.

On Monday, April 18,1983, I arrived at the embassy at 8:10 a.m. The nearby sidewalk parking was completely full, so I parked my car three blocks away from the embassy and walked toward the embassy.

It was showering, and the sky was gray, and a cold breeze was touching my face. I looked toward the consular entrance; it was full of applicants. And I figured out that it would be a long hectic day. It was a hectic Monday; when it was almost midday, the consular's entrance door was already closed. I received a telephone call from the main gate asking permission for a Mr. Hamo to submit his passport.

I got the permission, and I met him at the main entrance and accompanied him to the consular section. Poor guy—he had had a rough day, crossing from East to West, and after a polite apology from me, I processed his case and asked him to sit in the waiting room. After a while, I perceived a brilliant white light, disoriented about my location. My right eye opened, but the left one was obscured by mud. Beneath the cabinets, I found myself amidst fire and destruction, experiencing intense pain. Attempts to cry for help were hindered by blood flowing from my mouth. Struggling to loosen my necktie,

Diplomat, Without Portfolio

I witnessed Dundas and Hamo attempting to pull my legs. After a while, I saw hospital lights above my head. Someone was washing my head with cold water. I saw Marianne over my head and asked, "What are you doing here?"

My voice was weird, and I didn't remember anything after that.

I opened my eyes, and TV journalists were filming me and the Lebanese minister of foreign affairs, Mr. Elie Salem, along with the former minister of tourism, Mr. Souren Khanamirian. All were in my room talking to my wife.

Astonished, I tried to talk, but no voice came out. And Marianne asked me not to try to. I had a terrible headache and felt that my head was wrapped fully. I asked myself, "What is this?" I got no answers.

After almost three to four days, I was awake, and Marianne was beside me, holding my hand. I asked her, with hand sign, to give me a pen so that I may ask questions in writing.

Marianne burst into tears at that moment. While crying, she pronounced the names of my colleagues—Kamal, Shahe, Souad, Yolla and Tony—and said that they perished. She said it was an explosion, and I had been saved.

Marianne, family members, and friends were everyday visitors at the hospital. After my hospitalization at AUH (American University Hospital), my uncle who did not cross to West Beirut during the whole civil war period sacrificed himself. He wanted to carry me with his car back home from the hospital.

After almost a month and my discharge, my return home was like returning from the holy pilgrimage. Besides my family members, relatives, friends, and classmates, all our neighbors were in front of our building, waiting for my arrival.

Being an Armenian and traditionally very tight with the family, I was supposed to hug and kiss every single person at the entrance, and then I was supposed to leap over the sheep slaughtered under my feet to keep the devil far away from our home.

During the whole period during my stay at home and until my travel to Boston for further operations, Marianne and my parents and close relatives were always beside me and taking care of me. The tight and close relationship between the members of the traditionally close Armenian families echoed and obviously showed about their care and interest in my health and future activity.

My close relatives and friends were concerned about my safety and future. They advised me to leave my consular job.

I continued to work while having continuous eight surgeries and working even as far in Yemen and in Athens, Greece, as a liaison officer between Beirut and Athens. This was where as a foreign service national employee I proved my professionalism, expertise, and devotion to my duty and supervised even diplomats who were working under my supervision.

I was awarded Best Foreign Service Employee of the Year 1987, and it was the source of a big pride for me and my family members.

Marianne never complained; she was beside me always. But the children were always unhappy with my work and travel plans. I used to make plans during their vacations and summer seasons to join me and to spend more time with me while I was on duty far from home.

DIPLOMAT, WITHOUT PORTFOLIO

FADE IN:

AERIAL SHOT - Daytime, gray sky and rainy day.
From seaside, approaching toward the coast of Beirut, Corniche Beirut, Rue de France, and Ain el-Mreisseh.

There is a large demonstration in front of a huge U-shaped seven-floor building. Hundreds of people are marching and chanting in front of the building.

Local Internal Security Forces are guarding the 2 entrances of the building and the corniche around the building.
Shutters of the building are all closed.
Black Ford van is parked in the alley of the building.
A US flag is in the middle of a small garden in front of the building.

Banners - Americans go home! Americans leave us alone! (Arabic and English) People are singing, shouting, and showing their arms to the building and crossing in front of the building.

FADE OUT:

FADE IN:

EXT - Noontime, Beirut, JFK Street, the same day. The sky is gray, and rain is pouring.
Taxi stops.
BA opens his umbrella while he is in the taxi and jumps out and hurries down toward the Ain Mreisseh seaside area.
Umbrella open in his hand and a folder in his second hand, he runs down through the wide steps between JFK Street and Ain Mreisseh. His trench coat becomes wet. He approaches a huge building.

ISF GUARD
EXT - Fat, tall ISF guard, raindrops falling from upper part of his trench coat. He stops BA with his hand.
Where are you going? (In Arabic)

BA
I have an employment interview in the embassy.

ISF GUARD
What!

Guard looks to BA's situation and is astonished, pauses a little bit and then points his right-hand finger and indicates the entrance of the building and continues (In Arabic).
Go! Go!

EXT - BA runs toward the alley and rings the bell at the entrance of the building.
The door opens.

INT - BA inside the building of the US embassy in Beirut.
Post One in the lobby at the entrance of US embassy.
Looks right and then to the left. Marine guard behind a glassed room indicates the other side of the entrance with his finger.

GHATTAS, RECEPTION DESK
(Noticing BA)
Can I help you, sir?

BA
INT – In the lobby, while cleaning himself and wiping his face and head and trench coat with his handkerchief.
I have an appointment to see Mr. Paul, sir.

GHATTAS, RECEPTION DESK
What's your name, sir?

> BA

BA, sir.

> GHATTAS, RECEPTION DESK
> (Pulls the phone and collects numbers while talking to BA)

One second, sir.

> (Ghattas talks on the phone)

Mr. BA is here to see Mr. Paul.

> (Ghattas approves the conversation with his head movement)

Okay, I will.

> (Ghattas talks to BA)

They are coming to pick you upstairs, sir.
Have a seat, sir.

> BA
> (Jumps from his chair and approaches the reception desk and then goes back to his seat)

Thank you.

INT - BA looks around, cleans his face and head. Checks the reception desk while watching Marines Post 1, reception.
A lady approaches the reception desk. She picks a form from Mr. Ghattas at the reception desk.

> GHATTAS, RECEPTION DESK

Indicating the lady, requests BA to accompany her to the upper floor.
> Sir, please accompany the lady.

> CA, EMPLOYEE

Good afternoon, sir.
Please follow me.

INT - BA walking with CA, accompanies her to the upper floor.
All the shutters of the upper-floor offices are closed.
BA salutes the sitting and walking employees by just moving his head.
CA, smiling, indicates an empty chair and asks BA to sit.

>CA, EMPLOYEE
>Have a seat, sir.

INT - CA knocks on the door of an employee and enters.

>CA, EMPLOYEE

Returns and invites BA to the same room. She introduces BA to Mr. Paul.
>Mr. Paul, this is Mr. BA.

>PAUL
>(Stands up behind his desk stretches his hand toward BA)
>Good afternoon, Mr. BA. We were waiting to meet you. How are you?

>BA
>Thank you, sir. I'm fine.

BA tries to locate a place to put his wet trench coat.

>PAUL
>(Indicates the second empty chair in front of his desk and asks BA to put his trench coat there)
>You can put it there.
>(Paul apologizes for the shutters and darkness of the room while checking some papers on his desk.)
>Sorry. For security reasons, we are keeping the shutters down. Palestinians had a demonstration in front of the embassy half an hour ago.

> BA

Stunned and frozen, just looks and follows the conversation.

> PAUL (Cont.)
>
> I see you have a good experience in various firms, and you would like to join and help us.

> BA
>
> Yes, sir. If you give me that chance and the opportunity.

> PAUL
> (He smiles, looking into BA's eye)
>
> Yes. If you qualify with the requirements, why not?
> Have you ever been a member of any organizations, Mr. BA?

> BA
> (BA looks innocent and suspicious, and moving his head right and left, instantly answers.)
>
> No, sir!

> PAUL
> (His eyes on the form.)
>
> I read here, you are a member of Ardavast Theater?
> What kind of a group is this, and who are the directors?

> BA
> (A little bit relaxed)
>
> Oh yes. These are young Armenian directors and schoolmates. They studied in Armenia, and we like theater, and we perf——

> PAUL
> (Interrupts BA's conversation with eyes still on the papers)
>
> I see you like acting.

BA
(Moving his head forward)
Yes, sir!

PAUL
To which local Armenian party belongs this Ardavast Theater?

BA
(Looks directly into the eyes of Paul)
This belongs to "Armenian Young Generation Cultural Union." But we don't see the representatives of the Union. We learn our script and then act together at Gulbenkian theater, and we perform a couple of times each show.

PAUL
(Looks to the eye of BA)
In which show have you acted last time?

BA
Relaxed and a smile on his face
The Kitchen of Monica Ali, sir. My role was one of the cooks. "One note to her ear." Molière, I was one of the soldiers.

PAUL
Smiling, reads other parts of the form. And he relaxes, pushing his chair backward.
Why you would like to work at the US embassy?

BA
(Looking sharp and to the eyes of Paul)
Sir, since my childhood, I was fond of USA, and I was watching US movies and wearing jeans and cowboy shirts, and I was westernized, even without seeing USA.
I read about USA in high school. We talk a lot about the achievements of USA. I like USA. It's democratic and free

Diplomat, Without Portfolio

country. I would like to join the embassy and work and, at the same time, learn a lot.

> PAUL
>
> While sitting, he approaches his chair at the desk.
> What do you mean with *we*?

> BA
> (Relaxed and his eyes widely open and his hands flying in the air)
> Oh! I mean my friends". (Pause) Classmates, sir. (Pause) At home, they know me. I like the western music. I hear always Voice of America. I play guitar, western music.

FADE OUT

FADE IN:

INT - BA accompanies Paul, and they enter a well-decorated suite in the embassy with a US flag behind the desk. A person sitting behind his desk, his eyeglasses on his nose, jumps from his chair, seeing Mr. Paul. In a loud tone, he welcomes Paul and looks controlling BA.

> PAUL
> While smiling
> Mr. Morgan, this is Mr. BA, and this is his folder.

> MR. MORGAN
> While standing behind his desk, clips his eyeglasses, thanks Paul, and looks controlling BA and shakes his hand. He asks BA to sit in the chair in front of his desk. Paul leaves the room.
> Welcome to the consulate, Mr. BA. I'm glad that you made it.

BA
(Swallowing his saliva, and very politely.)
Thank you, sir, having me today.

MR. MORGAN
(Sits on a chair in front of his desk, facing BA)
I visited Armenia, and I'm impressed that your countrymen there are already westernized before their neighbors. They are clever and hard workers too.

BA
(Watches Morgan and relaxes)
Yes, sir. Thank you.

MR. MORGAN
Relaxed, he pulls a cigarette (Salem) from his soft box and puts it in the pipe. He lights the cigarette and continues his conversation.

What we are looking for is an ambitious young employee who is a hard worker and energetic, who can work under stress and pressure.

Here, we deal with the public and handle visa processing—various kinds of visas and citizenship cases.

We are in need of fresh blood to our visa section, where already we have employees almost at the age of retirement.

(He stretches himself and puts his eyeglass on his nose and reads part of the application and looks directly at BA and continues talking.)

I read your application, and I'm impressed that you have a good experience as an accountant with your previous employers. Plus, you indicate that you handle and deal with various kinds of documents.

Also, you speak various languages.

This is what we need in this section.

(Continues to read and stops)

>All right! I will inform the result of our interview to Mr. Paul, and they will let you know about the procedures.
>I'm satisfied with your employment application.
>
>>BA
>>(Astonished and lost with innocent appearance)
>>Thank you very much, sir. Thank you!

INT – BA, accompanied by the pretty secretary, reaches the main entrance of the embassy and thanks her.

>>BA
>>Thank you.

EXT - BA leaves the building.

FADE OUT:

FADE IN:

MAY 15, 1973

INT - A big crowded room with three employees typing and interviewing applicants, sound of typewriters around and BA working behind his desk.
BA typing and a Lebanese family sitting in front of his desk.

>>BA
>>(BA talks to a man sitting in front of his desk)
>>Is this your brother's address in US?
>
>>APPLICANT
>>(Pulling a piece of paper from his big envelope)
>>Yes, sir. This is the complete address.

> BA
> How many children do you have, all together?

> APPLICANT
> Six, sir.

> BA
> All right. Visas are typed and ready now, and the consular officer will interview you.

INT – BA carries folders to the adjacent room.

INT – Red-haired American officer wearing a dark suit invites the family to his room.

> SETON
> (Consular officer stands up and raises his right hand and asks the family to raise their right hand too.)
> Raise your right hand.
> (Arabic translation by BA)
> Do you swear that all your statements—what you had written and what you will say to me today—are true to the best of your knowledge?

> APPLICANT
> (Looks at BA and the consular officer.)

> BA
> (Translates in Arabic the statement of the consular officer)

> SETON
> BA, are the names matching to the passport?

> BA
> Yes, sir.

Diplomat, Without Portfolio

SETON
(Checking typed papers and envelopes)
Why you would like to immigrate to the US?

BA
(Translates into Arabic)

APPLICANT
(Speaks Arabic)

BA
(Translates into English)
Sir, everywhere is war in South, and I will take my children to a country where they can join their uncle and can live and study freely and continue their life in a better environment.

SETON
I understand.
All right. I see your papers are in order and will issue and deliver your visas today.
Congratulations. (In Arabic) *Mabrouk!*
(He delivers the signed papers and folders to BA.)
(BA translates into Arabic)

APPLICANT
(Stands up and begins to cry, approaching the US flag. He Kisses the US flag.)
Thank you! Thank you, sir!
(Applicant shakes the hand of the consular officer and tries to kiss the hand of the Officer.)

SETON
No, no. Be happy in USA. Good luck to you all.
Make sure your children study in US.
(He withdraws his hand while laughing.)

>   BA
>   (BA indicating the door with his hand)
>   Say thank-you and let's go to my room.
>   This way, this way.

INT - BA takes the family out of the consular officer's room.

FADE OUT:

FADE IN:

MARCH 15, 1975

EXT - Early sunny afternoon, streets deserted, cars running from left to right and vice versa. There are civilians, rifles in their hands, on each street corner and some Lebanese Internal Security Forces just regulating the empty streets and trying to help the citizens pass from one area to the other.

EXT – Late afternoon.

BA driving his Opel car alone.

>   BA
>   (Astonished, approaches with his car to the one of
>   the ISF people. He speaks in Arabic.)
>   Shou fi, shou fi yaa shabab.
>   (What's going on, what's going on guys.)

EXT - One of the ISF group in front of an armored vehicle speaks in Arabic.

>   ISF MAN
>   It's better run to your house. It seems the situation is very tense!

EXT – Explosion of a nearby bomb shakes the area.

> BA
> (Covers his head with his hands)
> Shukran…shukran, ya shabab.
> (Thank you…thank you, guys.)

EXT - BA drives his car very fast.
EXT - BA arrives at his house and parks his car in front of a building.

INT - He enters his apartment.

> BA
> Hi, darling.
> (BA kisses his wife and sits in front of the TV set in a room.)
> See what's going on.
> (BA murmurs alone)
> What is this?

INT - The TV speaker indicates confrontation in many parts of Beirut and gunmen in the streets.
Christian gunmen clashing with various civil-dressed people.

TV - People are advised to stay at home. Do not leave your houses, and keep away from Damascus Street.

INT - Two MPs on TV dispute that the shooting on the bus will not pass easily, and this will have many negative impacts and will create various problems and divisions between the Lebanese and non-Lebanese.

INT – At the same time, the TV indicates the location and shows scenes of a bus with flattened tires and a lot of bullet holes all over the bus. There are bloodstains on the seats and on the ground near the bus.

> BA
> (Astonished and lost, looks to Marianno.)
> This is what we want now in our country!

INT - Frozen period of 5 seconds, the voice of the TV goes down.
INT - BA picks the phone adjacent to his seat and calls the numbers on the phone.

> BA
> (Astonished and worried)
> Your Excellency, how are you?
> What is this?

> VOICE FROM OTHER SIDE
> Are you at home?

> BA
> Yes, yes. I just arrived.

> VOICE FROM OTHER SIDE
> Stay at home!
> Do not move. It is a dangerous situation.
> It's all over the whole part of the city and maybe the whole country.

> BA
> (Looking toward TV and worried)
> What do you say?

> VOICE FROM OTHER SIDE
> Yes! Yes! BA, take care of the family.
> Plan to stay at home for a week or two, and stock food at home.

> BA
> Really? Unbelievable!

                    VOICE FROM OTHER SIDE
Yes, BA. We are busy to arrange a ceasefire, but it is very difficult.
Talk to you later.
Keep the family safe, all right?

                    BA
                    (BA is completely astonished and worriedly turns to Marianno.)
Marianno, this is unbelievable. This is real, and this is bad news.
It seems these people, they lost their mind, and they want to control this country.
All he mentioned is that it will take a long period, and I have to plan to stay at home for a week or two.

                    MARIANNO
What?
Leave it to God. We don't know.
But as he said, plan to stay at home and be safe.
God knows what's going on in the streets. That's why he instructed you to do so.
Let me call the parents and inform them.

INT - BA continues to listen to the TV while Marianno picks the phone and calls the numbers on the phone.

FADE OUT:

FADE IN:

FEBRUARY 15, 1976

Ext - Afternoon in Beirut. Roadblock with sands and iodized barrels.

BA is driving his green Opel Rekord car, and five other employees are in the car.
BA approaches the roadblock, and a group of gunmen with Kalashnikovs stops the green car.

>BA
>Marhaba yaa shabab!
>(Hello, guys!)
>>(One of the militia members talks with BA.)

>GUNMAN
>Marhaba! Where are you heading?
>>(He is looking inside the car.)

>BA
>>(Innocently and politely)
>Heading home, Bourj-Hammoud!

>GUNMAN
>All of you, Bourj-Hammoud? Armenians!

>BA
>>(With his hand indicating all the passengers)
>Yes, sir. We are all Bourj-Hammoud, Armenians.
>You eat *basturma* like us, right?
>>(BA delivers a small package of basturma to the gunman.)

>GUNMAN
>>(While staring inside the car)
>Okay, go! Go! Basturma!
>You Armenians are our friends.

>BA
>>(While driving the car, he turns backward.)
>See? A white lie and a piece of basturma saves your life.

This is not a visa line!

> EDMOND
> (Old man, a colleague)

Thank you, BA. You always saved our life.
You think he did not notice that we are not Armenians?

> BA

As long as he is going to eat basturma now, he will not even remember me.
Next time, I will tell him both your mothers are Armenians.

> NABIL
> (Young man a colleague)

Friends, let's talk seriously!
If this situation will continue like this, I'm planning to resign.

> ELIAS
> (Bold old man sitting in front seat in between BA and Shahe, another young employee)

Hey! Wait a couple of weeks. Things will be settled.

> SHAHE
> (Young man sitting in front-seat passenger side near the window)

Weeks! Don't you see? This is the beginning of the war.
This will last months if not years.

EXT - Driving the car and watching every single crossing and streets.

> BA
> (Speaks loudly)

All right! All right!
You all became politicians here.
Don't you notice? We are in the middle of war, and I don't see any ending here.

As long as the Palestinians are outside of their camps, there is no peace here.
Prepare yourself, gentlemen, for a long war.

EXT - BA slows down his car and stops in a corner of a deserted street.

          BA
Here we come.
          (BA laughs and indicates the corner.)
Stop No. 1.
          (Two employees step out of the car.)

          EDMOND
Drive safe, BA. See you tomorrow.

          BA
All right! See you at six tomorrow.

FADE OUT:

FADE IN:

EXT – LATE AFTERNOON, STILL LIGHT IN THE SKY
"Kalb River" sign covers the scenery.
BA drives his Opel car with Marianno next to him on passenger seat. Lebanese ISF roadblock stops BA. Guard indicates with his hand the right side of the street for ID check.
BA slowly approaches the ISF officer and stops his car. Both BA and Marianno are sitting in the car.

          ISF OFFICER
          (Looking toward BA and then Marianno)
Your ID please.

> BA
> (BA collects from Marianno her ID and hands his and her documents to ISF officer.)
> These are our IDs.

> ISF OFFICER
> (Tries to read and tries to indicate something)
> What is this?

> BA
> (While seated in the car, grasping the IDs, he tries to explain.)
> This is my ID from the American embassy.
> And this is my wife's Soviet passport.
> She has no Lebanese ID yet. We are newly wed.

> ISF OFFICER
> (Completely astonished and looks at BA and Marianno)
> What? What!
> One American and one Soviet, in the same car!
> Unbelievable. This is what we lack in this country?
> (Begins to laugh and indicates the street)
> What kind of a *makhlouta* (in Arabic, "mixture") is this?
> Go, brother. Go! Go!
> God with you.

> (ISF officer returns the documents to BA. BA starts his car and leaves laughing too.)

EXT – BA talks to Marianno while driving inside the car.

> BA
> See, darling? He was shocked and not even able to identify to which sect we belong.
> American and Soviet documents was enough to him so that he releases us.

>   MARIANNO
>   (Enjoying the trip)
> The officer noticed a blond girl and being foreigner, taught better to release rather than to interfere.

>   BA
> It seems so. We are lucky.
>   (While driving and paying attention to the line of stopped military vehicles)

FADE OUT:

FADE IN:

OCTOBER 1984

INT - MIDSUNNY DAY, a big hall, employees in various corners of the hall.
Three employees talking with each other, two secretaries typing on separate desks.

>   MARCO
>   (His left hand in casts and wrapped with blue hanger. With his right hand, he collects numbers on the phone.)
> Hi, BA. How are you today?
>   (Sounds shocked and tired)
> Good! Can you come to the ambassador's residence? He would like to see us together.

EXT - Early afternoon – sunny day.
Hillside of Beirut – ISF guards all over the streets and BA, driving a white Mercedes car, passes through two ISF roadblocks.

> BA
> (Approaches the first ISF roadblock)
> I'm trying to locate the US ambassador's residence.

> ISF OFFICER
> Are you an employee of the embassy?

> BA
> Yes, sir.

> ISF OFFICER
> (Checks ID)
> This way, sir.
>> (ISF officer gestures with his hand toward the residential area.)

EXT – BA, driving a white Mercedes car, arrives at the residential diplomatic corps area. There are different flags of various countries on various houses, and he locates the ambassador's residence with a US flag in front of the residence.
BA parks his car facing the residence, at the main entrance far from the iron main gate, and walks toward the house.

EXT - BA walks toward the residence and salutes the two ISF security guards. He shows his ID and advances toward the main entrance, the iron gate of the residence.

EXT – A guard, list of names in his hand, salutes BA with a smile.

> GUARD
> Good morning, BA.
> They are waiting for you.

EXT - BA also salutes group of guards in front of the gate by raising his palm.

> BA
> Good morning, Ahmed!

INT - BA rushes toward the inner entrance of the residence. A huge generator is at the right side of the entrance. Two additional guards at the inner entrance salute BA.
Marco meets BA at the entrance of the inner part of a long hall.

> MARCO
> (Smiling and shaking with left hand)
> Hi, BA. How are you?
> Come on in. Let's wait for the ambassador.

> BA
> All right, Marco. How do you feel?

> MARCO
> I'm all right. They casted my arm yesterday at the hospital. I have pain, but I'm okay.
> I'm staying with the ambassador here until things are settled.

INT - BA and Marco standing inside the hall, waiting to meet the ambassador.

> MARCO
> He wants to talk to us, especially to you. He asked me to call you. He wants to discuss with you certain things related to the consulate.

> BA
> (Looks around and salutes with his hand the other busy officers and working colleagues around him.)

INT - Embassy nurse Mounira, with white suit on her, approaches Marco. She is holding some pills in her hand, along with a glass of water.

MOUNIRA
Marco, time for your pills.
Please swallow these.
> (Delivers the pills and gives the glass of water to Marco)

MARCO
Thank you.
> (Marco gets the pills and the glass, and he swallows the pills while drinking the water.)

Still, I have pain, Mounira.

MOUNIRA
I'm sorry!
You need two to three weeks to feel better.
> (Nurse Mounira notices BA)

Hi, BA. How are you?
Thank God. You are lucky this time!
> (BA hugs the nurse and kisses her cheeks.)

BA
Thank God, Mounira!
I'm still alive, compared to others. We lost again eighteen colleagues.

INT – The ambassador's voice comes from the room next door, while he is chatting with an officer.
His palm is wrapped with white medical wraps.
He notices Marco and BA in the middle of the room, and he indicates with his hand to the officer that he is going to meet Marco and BA. The officer leaves, and the ambassador approaches BA and Marco.

BA
Mr. Ambassador!
How are you, and how do you feel?

> **AMBASSADOR BARTHOLOMIO**
> (Smiling and looks worried)
> Okay, okay, BA. We are strong and alive.
> > (He pauses three seconds, checking his wounded and bandaged palm. Nurse Mounira checks the palm.)
>
> **MOUNIRA**
> How are you today?
>
> **AMBASSADOR BARTHOLOMIO**
> Better than yesterday.
>
> **MOUNIRA**
> So this means no pills anymore?
>
> **AMBASSADOR BARTHOLOMIO**
> Yes. Yes please.
> > (Mounira leaves for the other end of the hall.

The ambassador puts his arms around the shoulder of BA and continues.

> BA, we still can work.
> I asked…
> > (Indicating Marco with his hand)
>
> and you to see me and discuss with me some details and see what we can do with these files and with the consulate operations.
> I'm getting requests every moment for visas and passport services.
> Also, I have to give an answer to the Department and the authorities here.
> BA, you have previous experience with this situation.
>
> **BA**
> (Looking the Ambassador in the eye)

Mr. Ambassador, we have to collect the files and the passports from the rebels first and then...

AMBASSADOR
And then what?

BA
(Looking at Marco)
Can we operate from the annex or the residence?

AMBASSADOR
Absolutely *no*! And *no*!

BA
(Thinks a short moment and initiates the conversation)
Then we have no other alternative, Mr. Ambassador!
We have to move the files outside of Beirut.

AMBASSADOR
Where to?

BA
I have only one choice where we have available space and can accommodate the whole files. Our applicants—both Moslems and Christians—can be served safely.
It's going to be Athens, Greece, sir.

AMBASSADOR
Athens? It's a perfect and good choice, BA!
(He raises his voice and, with his other palm, knocks the nearby table.)
Yes, yes, yes. I accept it!
(Looks happily to Marco and, with a loud voice, continues.)
Marco, please take note and make all the required connections and contact the Department and Athens.

Indicate that our first choice is to transfer the files to Athens.
> (Turns to BA)

BA, how many employees you think you need in Athens from Beirut?

BA

Mr. Ambassador, with me, three employees. And I can run the Beirut Files in Athens.

AMBASSADOR

With your past experience, are you sure, BA, that three employees are enough?

BA

Yes, sir! I can manage and operate with three.

AMBASSADOR

All right. Any other choice or suggestions, Marco?

MARCO

No, sir! We can rely on BA and his group, and we can operate from Athens.

AMBASSADOR

Good then.
> (Looking relaxed and addressing the question to BA)

How many employees do you need, BA, to collect and pack the files ready for shipment to Athens?

BA

(Satisfied)

I need three days, Mr. Ambassador, and at least four to five employees to help us and to pack the files in carton boxes.

AMBASSADOR

You got them, BA.

As of tomorrow, you will be in charge of the files and pack them.
Make your choice with Marco, and choose who you will take with you.
Get supplies, vans, whatever. And you have to be ready to fly to Athens.
    (Looking at Marco)
Work with BA, and make the arrangement. And ask GSO to prepare the travel orders to BA and his group, for after three days.

    MARCO
Yes, Mr. Ambassador!

One final question, sir.
What about the classified documents?

    AMBASSADOR
Marco, tie them to BA's hand, and let BA carry the box on his lap.
He has a clearance for that, right?

    MARCO
Yes, sir.

    AMBASSADOR
    (Shakes hands with BA with his wounded arm)
All the best, BA.
Do it fast. That's an order.
And bon voyage!

INT - Ambassador talks with other officers about different matters. BA rubs his head.

MARCO
(Marco, looking to BA)
It's an order now!
See who you can choose and plan. Think how we are going to wrap the whole files.

BA
(Surprised and astonished, pulls his eyebrows up)
Marco! Let me call my wife and inform her. Also...

MARCO
BA, phones are all busy from here and then...oh! There is no time.
Oh! One more thing. As you know, this decision is top secret. Except for your wife and chosen assistants, no one has to know about this decision.

BA
(Eyebrows up)
I got the point! Okay, Marco.
All right.
I will choose...
(Looking at Marco and relieved from the conversation.)

MARCO
(Laughing and relaxed)
BA, you are in charge now.
You are the boss!
You can choose and plan for anything now.
Organize your team, and plan for the collection of the files.

BA
(Astonished)
Oral promotion.
Okay! Okay! I will call my assistants from home.
I will call the security group to join me at Porfin Building.

Collect whatever we have there first.
And then we will finalize the collection of remaining documentation from annex, the bombed Aoukar building.
And be ready to go.
(BA shakes Marco's hand and hugs him.)
All right, Marco.
I'll see you…maybe in Athens!
You will come to visit us.

MARCO
(Tears in his eyes)
I assure you, BA.
I will come to visit the group on my way to DC.

EXT - BA leaves. While passing through a group of bodyguards, he salutes them by hand and shakes the hands of some guards.
He leaves the residence and walks toward his parked Mercedes car.
BA opens the door and sits in his car, and he takes notes.

BA
His head in his hands and leaning to the stir, he speaks to himself while he is watching the ISF checkpoint facing his car.
(BA's voice, talking to himself)
Oh my god!
What is this?
A new page in my life.
I have to leave the family and operate at the embassy in Athens. And where is the ending? Open assignment.
God knows how many months.
Maybe years. No one knows.
Ambassador did not even say for how many months!
(Pauses five seconds)

EXT - BA starts his car and drives toward the ISF roadblocks.

FADE OUT:

FADE IN:

EXT - BA parks his car in front of a building and rushes to the apartment.

INT - Opens the door of the apartment.

        BA
Marianne. Marianne. Rush, rush.
I have very important news and information to share with you.

        MARIANNO
        (Meets BA in a room, kisses BA)
Your order, sir!
        (While she laughs and salutes)
Yes, what's going on?

        BA
Listen!
Top secret.
We are moving the files to Athens. And within three days, I have to leave and establish the consular section in Athens.

        MARIANNO
        (Astonished, pushes herself backward to the nearby sofa)
What!
History repeats itself.
Once again?

        BA
Yes! Yes! Marianno.
        (Comforts Marianno)
What can I do? It's an order, and I have to follow it.

Diplomat, Without Portfolio

>Keep it low, and we will talk to the kids and the parents this evening.
>Make your plan, and after a while, you will come and join me there.
>Meanwhile, please prepare my luggage from now on.
>I have a limited time to prepare myself.

BA looks worriedly at Marianno, and she looks at BA, worried. There is no further conversation.

FADE OUT:

FADE IN:

INT – A ROOM FULL OF FILE CABINETS, TWO DESKS, AND A MICROFISH MACHINE ON THE BACKGROUND. THERE IS A VISA MACHINE ON THE DESK. THERE ARE FIVE EMPLOYEES—TWO FEMALES AND THREE MALES—IN THE PRESENCE OF TWO MARINE GUARDS. THEY ARE WRAPPING CARD FILES AND UNFOLDING FILES FROM THE FILE CABINETS WHILE BA IS GIVING THEM INSTRUCTIONS.

>EMPLOYEE
>(Showing a bunch of black books to BA)
>Where can I put these books?

>BA
>(Responding to the question of one of the employees)
>Yes! The statistics book and quota control book go with this file.
>(BA indicates a carton box, which is open)

BA gives the instructions while standing in the middle of the room.

> BA

Guys, once we finish the wrapping of these folders, we have to collect also those which are located at the annex, in Aoukar.

FADE OUT:

OCTOBER 14, 1984

FADE IN:

EXT – CLOUDY DAY, EARLY MORNING IN BEIRUT. TWO BLACK VANS APPROACH BEIRUT INTERNATIONAL AIRPORT.

BA IS SITTING IN THE SECOND ROW OF THE VAN. IN HIS LAP IS A HUGE BAG CHAINED TO HIS ARM.
THE EMBASSY BODYGUARD SITTING AT THE PASSENGER SEAT WATCHES THE FRONT AND RIGHT SIDE OF THE STREET.
TWO BODYGUARDS ARE AT THE BACK SEAT.
BA—SEATED IN THE SECOND ROW OF THE VAN, IN THE MIDDLE SEAT BETWEEN TWO FEMALE EMPLOYEES—TRIES TO LOCATE SOMEONE AT THE DEPARTURE SECTION OF THE AIRPORT ENTRANCE.

> BA

Here he is, Sarkis. Our man, Colonel Ghaffour, is waiting for us.

THE VANS STOP AND PARK IN FRONT OF THE ENTRANCE OF THE AIRPORT. TWO GUARDS FROM THE SECOND VAN JUMP AND APPROACH THE FIRST VAN. THEY OPEN THE DOORS OF THE FIRST VAN AND TRY TO SECURE THE EXIT FOR BEDROS AND THE TWO FEMALE EMPLOYEES.

> BA
> (Tries to leave the van after the first female employee. He thanks the driver and, holding the box tight with his two hands, jumps out of the van.)

Thank you, Sarkis. Patience and all the best to you.
Thank you, *Shabab*.
Colonel, good morning!

> COLONEL GHAFFOUR

Welcome, BA! Good morning!
Ahlan Shabab!
Good morning, ladies.
> (Colonel Ghaffour salutes the group and receives a folder from the bodyguard.)

> BODYGUARD

Colonel, these are the passports and airway tickets!
They are under your jurisdiction.
> (He and Colonel Ghaffour laugh)

> COLONEL GHAFFOUR

Thank you, *ya Shabab*.
This way, Mr. Bedros. Ladies.

Colonel Ghaffour leads the three passengers toward the departure lounge of the airport.

EXT - BODYGUARDS UNLOAD SOME PERSONAL LUGGAGE FROM THE SECOND VAN. AFTER LOADING IT ON A CARRIAGE, THEY PUSH IT TOWARD THE DEPARTURE AREA.

INT – COLONEL AND BA WALKING TOGETHER WHILE THE TWO LADIES FOLLOW THEM AND THE TWO

GUARDS PUSH THE LOADING CARRIAGES TOWARD THE CHECK-IN AREA.

FADE OUT:

FADE IN:

INSIDE THE AIRCRAFT, COLONEL GHAFFOUR BRINGS THE ENVELOPE WITH PASSPORTS AND AIRWAY TICKETS AND DELIVERS THESE TO ONE OF THE LADIES AND SALUTES BA.
BA IS IN THE MIDDLE OF THE ROW WITH THE BOX ON HIS LAP. HE SALUTES WITH HIS RIGHT HAND, THANKING COLONEL GHAFFOUR.

> COLONEL GHAFFOUR
> Mr. BA, everything is in order.
> Have a good flight.
> Ladies!
> Safe Arrival.
> Without any invitation, I will see you in Athens.

> BA
> Colonel, thank you for everything.
> All right, I will see you there.

COLONEL GHAFFOUR LEAVES THE AIRCRAFT, AND AS THE DOOR OF THE AIRCRAFT CLOSES, THE STAIRS ARE WITHDRAWN FROM THE AIRCRAFT.

THE AIRCRAFT LEAVES THE AIRPORT, AND IT'S IN THE SKY.

FADE OUT:

FADE IN:

EXT-ATHENS AIRPORT- VIP LOUNGE
BLACK US OFFICER WALKS TOWARD THE ARRIVAL TARMAC.
AIRCRAFT APPROACHES TOWARD THE HUB.
THE DOOR OF THE AIRCRAFT OPENS, AND THE STAIRS APPROACHES TOWARD THE AIRCRAFT.
BA, WITH THE BOX IN HIS HANDS, DESCENDS THE STAIRS OF THE AIRCRAFT. TWO LADIES ACCOMPANY HIM.
AT THE TARMAC, THE BLACK LADY HUGS BA.

          MONIC
Hi! Welcome, BA.
You still look young and handsome.

          BA
Thanks, Monic! How are you?
This is Hind, and this is Salam.
      (BA introduces his assistants)

          MONIC
Hi, ladies. Welcome to Athens.
      (Bodyguard indicates the car parked at Tarmac.)

EXT - THE SOUND OF THE AIRCRAFT ENGINE AT THE BACKGROUND IS ON. BA AND MONIC TALK, AND THEY ALL WALK TOWARD THE BLACK AMERICAN CAR PARKED AT THE TARMAC.

FADE OUT:

FADE IN:

INT – CONSULAR SECTION OF THE US EMBASSY, ATHENS.

BA, MONIC, AND THE TWO LADIES WALK INSIDE THE CONSULAR SECTION. VARIOUS EMPLOYEES SALUTE BA AND THE LADIES.

>   MARY D
> Welcome! Welcome!
> Hi, BA. After so many years, one more time.
> You are changed.
>   (Mary D hugs BA and salutes the two ladies.)

>   FOTINI F
> Hi, BA. Welcome!
> Welcome, ladies!
>   (Fotini hugs BA and kisses the two ladies.)

INT - CONSULAR SECTION OF THE US EMBASSY, ATHENS. MONIC WALKS IN THE CONSULAR SECTION TOWARD A ROOM THAT LOOKS TOWARD THE GARDEN OF THE EMBASSY. SHE INFORMS A GENTLEMAN THAT THE GROUP FROM BEIRUT ARE PRESENT.
BA AND THE TWO LADIES FOLLOW MONIC AND ENTER THE ROOM.

>   MONIC
> So, Mr. Bill, this is BA and his group from Beirut.
>   (Monic indicates with her hand BA and the two ladies.)

>   BILL
>   (Stands up and, standing in front of the desk, salutes BA.)
> Hello, BA. Welcome to Athens.

Hello, ladies.
Have a seat please.
I understand you made it safely.
> (Bill indicates the chair and the seats in the room, and Monic and BA sit on the chairs in front of the desk, and the two ladies sit on the couch.)

    BA
Yes, Mr. Bill. Thank you for accepting and accommodating us.

    MONIC
Oh yes. Mr. Bill and me we worked hard to get the approval.

    BILL
    (Laughing loudly)
Yeah. Me and Monic, we hit the Department, convincing them that we can handle the whole operation.
Monic, knowing you and the past operation in Beirut with you, she was the first to approve that.

INT - A LADY ENTERS THE ROOM, AND SEEING THE GROUP, SHE SALUTES, NODDING TO BILL AND MONIC.

    ANN
Can I join you?
So this is Beirut Files staff!
Welcome! Hello. Hello.

    MONIC
Hi, Ann. This is BA, and this is Salam, and this is Hind.
> (Monic stands up, and she introduces the group to Ann. Ann, after saluting BA and the two ladies, sits between the two ladies on the couch.)

                    BILL
Good! Now that we are all here, let's jump and decide how we're going to proceed.
Monic, you will work with BA and show them where these people are going to operate, and then let's explain and discuss how we're going to proceed.

FADE OUT:

FADE IN:

INT – CONSULAR SECTION BEHIND THE INTERVIEW BOOTH.
BEDROS INTERVIEWS APPLICANTS BEHIND THE BOOTH AND INSTRUCTS THEM ON WHAT TO DO.
APPLICANT ALONE AT THE WINDOW, AND BEHIND HIM, THE WAITING ROOM OF THE CONSULAR SECTION, PEOPLE ARE SEATED.

                    BA
Let me have the instruction sheet and then the supporting documents.

                    APPLICANT
These are the consulate papers, and these are my passports, birth certificates, and marriage certificates.

                    HIND H
BA! Telephone call. An attorney from the US.

                    BA
BA LEAVES THE INTERVIEW BOOTH AND ENTERS HIS PRIVATE BOOTH. HE TALKS ON THE PHONE WHILE STANDING.

Hello! Good morning, sir.
Yes, sir. I'm in charge of the Beirut Files.
>(Pause)

Excuse me, are you the attorney of the record?
>(Pause)

Okay, how can I help you?
>(Pauses and he silently indicates with his eyes to Salam to add notation on the card.)

Okay then! Mail us the forms, and I will schedule him for final visa interview here in Athens, sir.
>(Pause)

Sure. Welcome, sir.

BEDROS RETURNS TO HIS INTERVIEW BOOTH AND CONTINUES TO TALK TO THE APPLICANT.

MONIC
SHE APPROACHES THE INTERVIEW BOOTH AND ASKS BEDROS TO APPROACH HER. SHE SHOWS A CLASSIFIED FILE TO BEDROS AND READS A COPY OF THE CABLE.

BA, we just got the cable from the Department and approval from Beirut.
They want to extend your stay here with indefinite assignment.

BA
Oh, Monic! I was predicting that after all these moves.

MONIC
You are here for a long while.
Call Marianno. Ask her to bring the children and join you.

BA
Yes, Monic. It seems so. I will.

MONIC
By the way, there is a new assignment to you.

Next week, you will be trained on the Wang system. And then you, in your turn, will train your group.
The Department will introduce the new automation system to the whole consulate.
The card system will be eliminated after that.
Be ready!

> BA

All right! All right!
Don't worry. I will manage that.
But I need five to six assistants as soon as the system is implemented.

> MONIC

All right! I will help you to locate and hire additional assistants for you locally. I will inform Mr. Bill too.

FADE OUT:

FADE IN:

INT- DAYLIGHT AT CONSULAR SECTION

MR BILL, ANN, AND MONIC ARE AT THE BACK OF THE INTERVIEW BOOTH, DISCUSSING THE PROCEDURES. BEDROS JOINS THEM, AND THEY DISCUSS THE NEW PROCEDURE INTRODUCED IN THE CONSULAR SECTION.
EVERY INTERVIEW BOOTH IS INSTALLED WITH A WANG PC, AND THE EMPLOYEES ARE WORKING AND SEARCHING THE INFORMATION THROUGH THE PCs.

> BA

Thank you, Mr. Bill and Ann. With this group now, we can eliminate the carding system.

Diplomat, Without Portfolio

ANN
Don't mention it, BA. We are obliged to produce this workforce for you.
Don't forget, you are lucky. We got the approval of our DCM to supply you with our assigned secretaries from the embassy and some dependents to accomplish your mission.
So they are all under your supervision, Bedros.

ANN INDICATES THE GROUP OF SIX EMPLOYEES IN A HALL, WHO ARE TYPING THE INFORMATION OF THE CARD FILES TO THE PCs.

BILL
I never figured out that a post like Beirut will have all these files.

BA
Wait, Mr. Bill, and you will see. Once we recreate the folders and cards which were destroyed during the incident, they will overpass Athens's files.

BILL
Good job! Congratulations. I'm surprised, BA, at your creative mind.

BA
Thank you, Mr. Bill. You too helped me along with my two favorite officers, a lot to achieve all these arrangements.
(BA turns first to Ann and then to Monic and, laughing, indicates to Bill.)
Also, I will thank both Monic and Ann, who helped me to accomplish this quick achievement.

MONIC
Don't mention it, BA! You have done all these.

                    ANN
Welcome, BA. These are the results of your hard work.

BILL, MONIC, AND ANN LEAVE THE AREA AND ENTER BILL'S ROOM.
BA APPROACHES THE SECRETARIES. HE CHECKS TYPED CARDS AND ANSWERS AND GIVES EXPLANATIONS.

                    BILL
Girls, do you think what I think?

                    ANN
Rewarding BA for his job.

                    MONIC
I say Best Foreign Service of the Year Award.

                    BILL
Good choice, Monic. I will work on it, and he is our nominee of the year 1987.
I will inform the ambassador. And from my side, case approved, ladies.

THE THREE OFFICERS AGREE AND SALUTE EACH OTHER.

FADE OUT:

FADE IN:

INT. DAYTIME – SUNNY DAY. INSIDE THE CONSULAR SECTION IN ATHENS, GREECE.

A SIREN GOES ON IN THE CONSULAR SECTION. PANICKED EMPLOYEES HERE AND THERE TRY TO WRAP

DOCUMENTS AND FOLDERS AND PASSPORTS FROM THE DESKS AND LOCK THEM IN THE FILES.

> MARINE GUARD
> (Shouting loudly and running to the end of consular section)
> Out! Out! Leave the section! Rush! Rush! Out!

SOME ALREADY RUN TOWARD THE EXIT CENTERS AND LEAVE THE CONSULAR SECTION. EMPLOYEES ARE CURSING. SOME ARE CRYING, SHOUTING, AND RUNNING TOWARD THE EXITS.

> BA
> (Like an experienced soldier)
> Girls, quick. Run towards the exits. Collect everything from desks and then run. Don't stay, Hind, Salam. You have to run! Now, now!

WITH HIND CRYING, SALAM CURSING AND CRYING, BOTH RUN WITH THE OTHER CONSULAR EMPLOYEES TOWARD THE EXITS.

> SALAM
> We ran away from the ghost town, and now we are facing new hell.

> HIND
> They reached us up to Athens. Run, Salam!

> BA
> (While running with Hind and Salam)
> My God, save us! What is this?

INT – EXTERIOR OF THE BUILDING

A HUGE GROUP OF EMPLOYEES—FEARFUL, SURPRISED, AND BREATHLESS FROM RUSH—LEAVE THE MAIN BUILDING, SOME RUNNING AND SOME WALKING QUICKLY. THEY GATHER AT THE PARKING LOT OF THE EMBASSY COMPOUND.
BEDROS, SALAM, AND HIND HUG EACH OTHER AND COMFORT EACH OTHER.
NATIONAL EMPLOYEES AND OFFICERS COMFORT EACH OTHER AND TRY TO HELP BY OFFERING WATER AND HELP TO EACH OF THOSE WHO SUFFERED, TO SEAT THEM ON THE PARKING SIDEWALK AREA.

(Thirty minutes later...)

AN OFFICER APPROACHES FROM THE BUILDING AND JOINS THE GROUP AT THE PARKING LOT.

> OFFICER
> (Shouts to the crowd)
> Okay, guys! Just a bomb threat!
> The security people are handling the case. They will let us know when we can go back to the offices once everything is clear.

THE WHOLE CROWD IS ASTONISHED. SOME CURSE AND SOME PUT THEIR PALMS TO THEIR HEADS AND SOME TO THEIR MOUTHS. RELIEVED AT THE NEWS, THEY COMFORT EACH OTHER.

FADE OUT:

FADE IN:

EXT – DARK EVENING, EMPTY STREETS. A MILITARY JEEP APPROACHES AND ENTERS THE ALLEY OF

THE AMERICAN EMBASSY'S POLICE STATION. TWO POLICEMEN OPEN THE BACK DOORS OF THE JEEP AND CARRY SOME CARTON BOXES TOWARD THE STATION. THE POLICE INSIDE THE STATION RECEIVES AND TRIES TO LOAD THEM ABOVE THE IRON CABINETS INSIDE THE BUILDING.

IND – A DIMLY LIGHTED ROOM, AROUND A ROUND TABLE, WALLS DECORATED WITH POSTERS OF FIGHTERS. A GROUP OF FIVE PEOPLE MEET SECRETLY IN AN ANONYMOUS LOCATION. TWO PERSONS, BESIDES IMAD MOUGHNIEH, CONVINCE, WITH DETAILS ON THE MAP, A YOUNG GUY TO PERFORM THE BIGGEST MISSION FOR ALLAH.

IND – A FLUORESCENT-LIGHTED ROOM IN A CLOSED GARAGE AREA. TWO PERSONS IN MECHANIC SHIRTS AND MILITARY PANTS FINALIZE TO LOAD GAS CONTAINERS, PLASTIC BAGS, AND ELECTRONIC DEVICES IN A BLACK VAN.

FADE OUT:

FADE IN:

EXT – THE SKY IS BROWN. IT'S 8:05 AM AS BA APPROACHES THE EMBASSY BUILDING AND TRIES TO LOCATE A PARKING SPOT ON AVENUE OF "FRANCE." WEARING A LIGHT BROWN TRENCH COAT AND FULLY DRESSED, HE TRIES TO HURRY AND SOMETIMES RUNS TOWARD THE EMBASSY ENTRANCE. THERE IS A VISA LINE ON HIS LEFT SIDE. IT'S A LONG LINE.

Bedros Anserian

>BA
>(Enters his room and hangs his trench coat behind the door. He checks his daily schedule. He hears Shahe is speaking with Kamal. BA asks Shahe.)

Shahe, how many numbers distributed this morning?

>KAMAL
>(Just showing his head toward BA's room)

Good afternoon, Mr. Supervisor. *Oh, Quelle elegance!*

>BA
>(Checks his suit and is smiling at Kamal)

Oh, I know. I was late. We slept after midnight. We had a wedding party yesterday night.

>SHAHE
>(Enters the room)

We have already ninety people in the waiting room and as much as the same outside without numbers.

>BA

Okay, Shahe. I'm sure it's a busy day. Continue your interviews, and I will come and give you a hand.

FADE OUT:

APRIL 18, 1983

FADE IN:

INT – EMBASSY CHANCERY. THE CLOUDY CLIMATE IS OBVIOUS FROM THE WINDOW OF AMBASSADOR DILLON'S ROOM. AMBASSADOR DILLON, WEARING HIS SPORTS PANTS AND SHIRT, IS PREPARING HIMSELF TO QUIT.

Diplomat, Without Portfolio

INT – EMBASSY CHANCERY. TWO OFFICERS IN AN ISOLATED "AID" ROOM DISCUSS POINTS AND PREPARE THEMSELVES AND WALK TOGETHER AND LEAVE THE ROOM.

INT – SNACK BAR OF THE EMBASSY. A BIG HALL WITH TEN TABLES—SOME OF THEM EMPTY AND SOME HAVE ONE OR TWO EMPLOYEES LUNCHING.
TWO OFFICERS APPROACH A TABLE ON THE LEFT SIDE OF THE SNACK BAR AND MEET FOUR PEOPLE WITH THEIR FOLDERS IN THEIR HANDS, WHO ARE WAITING FOR THE TWO NEW OFFICERS.

           CHIEF
Thank you, gentlemen, for accepting our lunch invitation.
    (All of them laugh and take their seats.)
There is no need to indicate what we are facing these days. The Agency needs our opinion and report with great urgency. Let's go directly to our conclusions and finalize our statements.

EXT – DRIVER CESAR, IN FRONT OF THE EMBASSY ENTRANCE. HE IS INSIDE THE AMBASSADOR'S CAR AND RADIOS THE MOTOR POOL.

           CESAR
    (Radios the motor pool)
Ready for the drive.

           ANONYMOUS MOTOR POOL GUY
    (Answers back from the radio)
Roger! Clear to drive.

EXT – "ABOU IMAD" DRIVING A BLACK VAN WITH HIS LEFT HAND WHILE LOOKING TO A PIECE OF PAPER IN HIS RIGHT HAND AND MURMURING PARTS OF THE KORAN.

INT – CONSULAR SECTION, FILING ROOM AREA EMPLOYEES, IN AND OUT TOWARD THE INTERVIEW AREA. BA WITH A BUNCH OF VARIOUS PASSPORTS IN HIS HAND. IN THE LEFT CORNER OF THE ROOM IS AN EMPLOYEE WORKING ON A MICROFICHE. A SECOND EMPLOYEE IS STAMPING VISAS ON PASSPORTS. A THIRD EMPLOYEE IS FILING DOCUMENTS, AND A FOURTH EMPLOYEE IS CASHING MONEY AT A SMALL WINDOW.

          BA
          (Distributes passports to employees for various work)
Shahe, please finalize this bunch from Microfiche checkups.
          (Delivers bunch of ten passports to Shahe)
Yolla, please work with Souad to stamp visas to these passports.
          (Delivers a bunch of twenty passports to Yolla)

INT – CONSULAR SECTION, FILING ROOM AREA. A TELEPHONE RINGS, AND SECRETARY SOUAD ANSWERS.

          SOUAD
Yes, he is here.
          (Souad asks BA to answer the phone)
Reception, Post 1, they would like to talk to you.

          VOICE FROM THE PHONE
Mr. Hamo is here. He would like to go upstairs.

          BA
          (Looks to his watch and answers the voice)
Let me talk to him.
Hi, Hamo. What's going on? It's ten minutes after twelve. Where you have been?

> HAMO'S VOICE
>
> Sorry, BA. Missed the appointment. Just passed with fear the museum crossing and reached late to the consulate.

> BA
>
> Okay, I understand. But you will be the last to be interviewed. Give the phone to the receptionist. Let me talk to him.
> (Small interruption)
> All right, Ghattas. Let him come upstairs, and refer the case to me.

INT – WHILE BEDROS IS DISTRIBUTING PASSPORTS FOR WORK, TONY ENTERS THE ROOM. WITH A LOW VOICE AND TAPPING ON A TABLE, SOMEONE IS SINGING AT THE ADJACENT ROOM.

> BA
>
> Tony, you had your lunch?

> TONY
>
> Yes.

> BA
>
> How was your first day in the consular section?

> TONY
>
> So far, so good. Everything is smooth.

> BA
>
> Okay, perfect. So please continue to interpret with the consular officer, Mr. Dundass.
> And meanwhile, tell our friend Mr. Kamal…
> (Bedros smiles, looking toward the adjacent room and indicating Kamal)
> that singing and dancing in the section during the lunch hour is forbidden.

INT – THE PRESENT EMPLOYEES INSIDE THE ROOM ALL SMILE.

INT – CONSULAR OFFICER LISA—IN A DIFFERENT LOCATION IN BETWEEN THE ROOM AND THE DOOR—JUST CHATS WITH A LADY IN ARABIC AND DISCUSSES AN ESSAY FROM A BOOK.

>TEACHER
>Yallah, Liza. Next lesson, you will write in Arabic. Okay, *shattoura*! (Okay, brilliant!)

>LISA
>(Laughs and looks shyly at teacher)
>Leila, I will write the essay and show it to you after tomorrow.

FADE OUT:

FADE IN:

EXT – A BLACK VAN CIRCULATES ON THE SEASIDE CORNICHE AND APPROACHES THE EMBASSY CHANCERY AND ENTERS SLOWLY TOWARD THE ALLEY.

>DRIVER OF BLACK VAN
>Allahu Akbar. Allah Ou Akbar. Allah Ou Akbar.

EXT – INSIDE A WHITE JEEP, A MAN HOLDING A REMOTE CONTROL IN HIS HAND PUSHES THE RED BUTTON.

EXT – WHITE FLASH OF LIGHTNING, A HUGE EXPLOSION, THE BUILDING TREMBLES. HUGE FIRE AND BLACK SMOKE FROM SEASIDE VIEW. CARS IN THE AIR. PEOPLE ON THE CORNICHE KNEEL, AFRAID OF AN AIR STRIKE.

Diplomat, Without Portfolio

THE CAFÉ PEOPLE AT HAMRA STREET JUMP FROM THEIR CHAIRS.

>GROUP OF PEOPLE
>(In the middle of traffic and the main road of Hamra Street, people shout.)

Where? Where?
Shoufi? Shoufi? (What's going on, what's going on.
Tayyarran, tayyarran.(Airplanes, airplanes.)
No! Explosion, explosion. Big one!
But where?

EXT – THE SCENE FROM JOUNIEH. A HUGE MASS OF VOLCANO-TYPE BLACK SMOKE RISES FROM THE SEASIDE BUILDING.

EXT – A BLOND LADY, WHILE WALKING HER DOG AT THE CORNICHE NEAR THE AUH BEACH, FREEZES. SHE LEAVES HER DOG AND KNEELS TOWARD THE LIGHT POLE OF THE BEACH AND TAKES HER HEAD INSIDE HER HANDS.

>DIANNE
>(Murmurs)

Oh my god!
This is an attack on the embassy!

INT –LISA JUMPS UP AND FALLS ON HER HANDS, AND THE NOTEBOOK IN HER HAND FLIES IN THE AIR, IN DARK SMOKE.

INT – A LADY, WHILE WALKING IN THE INTERIOR CORRIDOR OF THE CONSULAR SECTION, JUMPS UP AND FALLS ON HER BACK WHILE SHOUTING.

ANGEL
What is this?
Hellllp! Someone?

INT – NADIA, WHILE IN THE ELEVATOR.

NADIA
(ENGULFED IN SMOKE, CRIES AND SHOUTS)
Oww! Oww! Cannot breathe! My head!
Please help me! Take me out! Take me Out.
(Breathes slowly while her head is falling to the front, slowly.)

Ext - A WHITE JEEP-TYPE CAR QUICKLY LEAVES THE SCENE AND THE EXPLOSION AREA. TWO PEOPLE INSIDE THE JEEP ARE LAUGHING AND CURSING.

EXT – CORNICHE AT SEASIDE NEAR THE EMBASSY BUILDING. CARS HIT EACH OTHER AT THE SEASIDE STREETS. AMBULANCES FROM RAOUCHÉ AREA RUSH IN THE STREETS TOWARD THE BUILDING. FIREFIGHTERS CROSS THE JAMMED TRAFFIC.

EXT – MARIANNO IS INSIDE A TAXI HEADING TO HER WORKSHOP. THE RADIO IN THE TAXI ANNOUNCES:

RADIO
(Flash. Breaking news. Alarm music.)
We were informed that a deadly huge explosion in West Beirut just happened this afternoon. Hundreds of casualties and many wounded.
Details as soon as we receive them.(Alarm music)

INT – PRESIDENTIAL PALACE. ASSISTANT SECRETARY DRAPER MEETING WITH PRESIDENT GEMAYEL IN A FRIENDLY MEETING AT THE PRESIDENTIAL ROOM.

Diplomat, Without Portfolio

THE HEAD OF PROTOCOL KNOCKS ON THE DOOR AND ENTERS. HE APPROACHES THE PRESIDENT AND MURMURS SOMETHING IN HIS EAR. THE PRESIDENT'S APPEARANCE CHANGES.

     PRESIDENT GEMAYEL
 What do you mean? Explosion at the American embassy? Who?

(ASSISTANT SECRETARY DRAPPER, STUNNED, STANDS UP WITH THE PRESIDENT, AND THEY LEAVE THE PRESIDENTIAL ROOM. THE PRESIDENT GIVES ORDERS IN THE LOBBY OF THE PALACE.)

 Prepare my own car. Now.

(PRESIDENT GEMAYEL SALUTES ASSISTANT SECRETARY DRAPPER IN FRONT OF THE PRESIDENTIAL PALACE, WHO CATCHES HIS DRIVER AND BODYGUARDS IN FRONT OF THE PALACE AND LEAVES.)

EXT – BREAKING NEWS IN ARABIC.
A WOMAN'S MOUTH TOWARD THE MICROPHONE, LEBANESE VOICE OF LEBANON RADIO STATION.
(MIXED WITH) A MALE SPEAKER AT THE LBC TV STATION IN LEBANON ANNOUNCES:

     RADIO STATION WOMAN'S VOICE
 A deadly huge explosion was the reason of the collapse of seven floors of the American embassy in West Beirut. Hundreds of casualties, dead and wounded, from the embassy personnel and the passersby.

     SPEAKER LBC TV STATION
 A deadly explosion this afternoon happened at the American embassy, West Beirut, which caused the collapse of the

facade of a seven-floor building. Casualties with hundreds dead and wounded from both embassy personnel and the visa applicants.

EXT - MIXED ANNOUNCEMENTS OF BBC MIDDLE EAST TV STATION AND CNN MIDDLE EAST BUREAU.

BBC MAN'S VOICE
Breaking news. We were just informed that a huge explosion took place at the chancery of the American embassy in West Beirut. We'll inform you of the details soon.

CNN WOMAN'S VOICE
...and caused tremendous damages to the chancery. Casualties with hundreds dead in the line of visa applicants. It is not clear yet if Ambassador Dillon survived from this explosion.

EXT – MARIANNE INSIDE THE TAXI, LISTENING TO THE VOICE OF LEBANON ANNOUNCEMENT.

VOICE OF RADIO VOICE OF LEBANON
Hundreds of casualties in the American embassy.

MARIANNO
(FROM THE BACK SEAT, STRETCHES HERSELF TOWARD THE TAXI DRIVER.)

What? This is where my husband works.
Please! Please! Driver, I need your help.
Take me to the embassy. Please!

(TAXI OCCUPANTS TRY TO COMFORT MARIANNO.)

EXT – SHOCKED PEOPLE AROUND THE EMBASSY BUILDING ARE IN THE MIDDLE OF THE STREETS. THEY WATCH THE INCIDENT AND TRY TO APPROACH THE

BUILDING, SOME CLEANING THEMSELVES FROM THE GLASS AND WOOD SHRAPNEL OF THE EXPLOSION.

INT – ADMINISTRATIVE OFFICER BARON AND SECURITY OFFICER SERGEANT REACH THE AMBASSADOR'S ROOM AND HEAR THE AMBASSADOR CRYING AND BEGGING FOR HELP.

>BARON
>Give me your hand, Ambassador!

(BARON AND SERGEANT AND A MARINE GUARD IN CASUAL CLOTHING PULL THE AMBASSADOR FROM THE EDGE OF THE OPEN FLOOR. THEY CLEAN ALL THE GLASS SHRAPNEL FROM HIS BODY. TWO MARINES ALSO REACH THE AREA FOR HELP.)

>SERGEANT
>Any wounds, Ambassador? you need to rest.

(SERGEANT CLEARS AN AREA AND RUSHES TO COMFORT THE AMBASSADOR.)

>AMBASSADOR
>Baron, Sergeant, please leave me here with the marines. You try to help those who need help!

INT - EMPLOYEES INSIDE THE ROOMS CRY, AND WOUNDED EMPLOYEES SEEK AN EXIT TO LEAVE THE BUILDING. SHATTERED BODIES ARE IN THE CORRIDORS.

INT – VISA APPLICANTS JUMP FROM THE FALLEN WALL OPENED AT THE BACK SIDE OF THE WAITING ROOM TO THE EXTERIOR OF THE EMBASSY BUILDING. SOME ARE CRYING AND SOME ARE WOUNDED. SOME EMBRACE EACH OTHER FOR SAFETY.

EXT – LEBANESE ISF, ALONG WITH AMERICAN MULTINATIONAL FORCES, CORDON THE WHOLE BUILDING. MILITARY CHOPPERS HOVER ABOVE THE EMBASSY. A MILITARY RED CROSS CHOPPER OF THE US NAVY LANDS IN THE AREA.

THERE IS PANIC AROUND THE EMBASSY AREA.

INT – DARK BLACK DEVASTATED ROOM, WITH FIRE IN SOME PARTS OF THE ROOM. WATER PIPES ARE FLOODING WATER TOWARD THE CEILING. CASUALTIES ARE EXHALING GASPING SOUNDS AND THEIR LAST BREATH.

INT - EMPTINESS, BLACK SMOKE, NO SOUND FOR FIVE TO SIX SECONDS.

    BA
(UNDER FILING CABINETS, COVERED WITH BRICKS AND SAND, MOVES SLOWLY AND SHOUTS)

    Helllp! Helllp!

(BLOOD POURS OUT OF HIS MOUTH. HE TRIES TO MOVE HIS RIGHT HAND BUT CANNOT MOVE IT. HE TRIES TO UNTIE HIS NECKTIE WITH HIS LEFT HAND.)

    Helllp!

INT – TWO PEOPLE ALONG WITH A MARINE REACH THE AREA AND HEAR BA BEGGING FOR HELP.

INT - DUNDAS AND HAMO PULL BA FROM HIS LEGS, AND BOTH CARRY BA LIKE A PIECE OF MUTTON TOWARD THE BACK SIDE OF THE BUILDING.

EXT - TWO EMBASSY GUARDS HANDLE BA FROM THE FIRST FLOOR TO THE GROUND SIDE OF THE BACK SIDE OF THE EMBASSY BUILDING, CARRYING HIM LIKE MUTTON, WHILE ONE OF THE ISF OFFICERS REACHES THE AREA AND HELPS, JUST CARRYING HIM ON HIS SHOULDER TO THE NEARBY AMBULANCE.

EXT - JOURNALISTS SURROUND THE AREA AND TAKE PICTURES.

EXT - RED CROSS PERSONNEL HANDLE THE BODY OF BA FROM THE ISF OFFICER, AND THEY PUT HIM IN THE AMBULANCE.

INT - HAMO JUMPS INSIDE THE AMBULANCE, ALONG WITH THE WOUNDED BA.
THE AMBULANCE LEAVES THE AREA WITH SIREN SOUNDS AND GREAT SPEED, ZIGZAGGING BETWEEN DIFFERENT AMBULANCES.

FADE OUT:

FADE IN:

EXT – FIVE TO SIX AMBULANCES REACH THE ENTRANCE OF THE AMERICAN UNIVERSITY HOSPITAL AT THE SAME TIME. THEY ARE CARRIED STRAIGHT TO THE EMERGENCY ROOM.

INT – INSIDE THE EMERGENCY ROOM, HAMO PUSHES BA'S STRETCHER WHILE SHOUTING AND ASKING HELP.

     HAMO
  Doctor! Doctor!

(PULLS HIS JACKET AND COVERS BA'S FACE WOUND WHILE PUSHING THE ROLLING STRETCHER IN THE CORRIDOR OF THE HOSPITAL.)

>I need a doctor here urgently! Doctor!

INT – TWO DOCTORS REACH THE AREA AND PULL THE ROLLING STRETCHER AND ASK HAMO.

>FIRST DOCTOR
>Who is he?

>HAMO
>BA! BA from the consulate.

>SECOND DOCTOR
>(Astonished)
>Our friend BA!

INT – BOTH DOCTORS CHECK THE WOUNDS OF BA. WHILE CHECKING THE WOUNDS, ONE DOCTOR GIVES THE ORDER TO CLEAN THE OPERATING ROOM.

>FIRST DOCTOR
>(Gets pair of scissors and gives it to Hamo, who is cleaning his own wounds.)
>Undress him quickly!

INT – THE TWO DOCTORS CONSULT WITH EACH OTHER WITH WORRIED FACES AND CONTINUE TO WALK TOWARD THE OPERATING ROOM.

INT- HAMO, WITH A BIG PAIR OF SCISSORS IN HIS HAND, CUTS ALL BA'S CLOTHING.

FADE OUT:

FADE IN:

EXT – THREE OLDER MEN RUN TOWARD THE EMBASSY BUILDING. ONE OF THE MEN, HOLDING HIS ID IN HIS HAND OVER HIS HEAD, RUNS TOWARD THE RESTRICTED CORDONED AREA.

          OLD MAN
(WHILE CRYING AND SHOUTING AND COLLAPSING)
    My son! My son BA is there!
    Let me pass, please.
    Give me permission, please.
    I beg you.

          ISF
(TRYING TO CALM THE OLD MAN)
    Father! Father! Calm down. You cannot go there.
    Go to the hospital. They were all carried to the hospitals.

EXT – TWO MEN COMFORT THE OLD MAN AND CARRY HIM FAR FROM THE SCENE AND THE DESTRUCTION OF THE AREA.

FADE OUT:

FADE IN:

EXT – PRESIDENT GEMAYEL ARRIVES AT THE SCENE IN FRONT OF THE EMBASSY, AND ALL THE SECURITY PEOPLE CORDON HIS OWN CAR. THE LEBANESE ARMY CHIEF MEETS HIM DIRECTLY, AND TOGETHER, THEY DISCUSS THE SITUATION AND MEET SURVIVING EMBASSY PERSONNEL.

EXT – ASSISTANT SECRETARY DRAPPER ARRIVES AT THE SCENE TOO AND WALKS TOWARD THE BUILDING, SURROUNDED BY BODYGUARDS. MRS. DRAPPER ALSO ARRIVES AT THE SCENE FROM THE OTHER SIDE OF THE BUILDING, AND THEY MEET AND EMBRACE EACH OTHER IN THE OPEN AIR, WITH BODYGUARDS AND ISF SOLDIERS CORDONING THEM.

FADE OUT:

APRIL 19, 1983

FADE IN:

EXT – BULLDOZERS ARE WORKING TO DIG AND CLEAN THE AREA. CRANES PULL FALLEN WALLS AND PARTS OF THE BUILDING. AMBULANCES SCATTERED AROUND THE BUILDING WAIT TO CARRY NEWFOUND CASUALTIES FROM THE REBELS.

EXT – AMBASSADOR DILLON, SURROUNDED BY BODYGUARDS AND ISF SOLDIERS, GIVES A SPEECH WHILE PRESS SECRETARY JOHN READS THE OFFICIAL STATEMENT AND EXPLAINS THE SITUATION.
JOURNALISTS, PRESS, AND CAMERAMEN SURROUND THE AMBASSADOR AND HIS AIDES.

>   JOURNALISTS
>   (All together in Arabic, French, and English languages)
>   Who are behind this attack?
>   Who do you think?
>   Do you know the group behind this?

>   JOHN
>   (Wounded officer tries to calm down the crowd of Journalists)
> We have no definite answer to your question, and we will wait until we receive the result of the investigations from the local authorities.
>
>   JOURNALIST
>   (All, once again, hurry in their questions)
> Do you know the identity of the attackers?
> Any particular person?
> May be you know who did it?
>
>   JOHN
> As I indicated previously, the embassy did not receive any threats. We leave to the local authorities to identify the attackers.
>   (Bodyguards try to secure the ambassador's passage, and John accompanies the ambassador)
> Thank you very much, gentlemen. We have to go. Thanks for coming, and we will let you know about the new developments as soon as we get them.
>   (John leaves)

EXT – BULLDOZERS CONTINUE THEIR WORK. A LADY SEATED ON ONE OF THE REBELS AND SURROUNDED BY SOME COLLEAGUES AND RELATIVES ANXIOUSLY WAITS TO LOCATE HER HUSBAND'S BODY.

>   JOURNALIST
> Sorry, lady. We know you are here and waiting to locate your relative's body.

          SETA
          (While crying and weeping)
Yes, I'm here since yesterday and waiting to locate my husband. He is an employee of the consular section. His name is Kamal. I hope they can locate him alive.
          (Seta continues to cry and weep while relatives try to comfort her.

FADE OUT:

SEPTEMBER 10, 1976

FADE IN:

EXT – THREE TABLES IN THE LOBBY OF THE AMERICAN EMBASSY. EMPLOYEES ARE REGISTERING FOREIGNERS AND AMERICAN CITIZENS. THREE BUSES ARE IN FRONT OF THE EMBASSY ON THE CORNICHE, FULL OF PASSENGERS. EMBASSY GUARDS CONTROL THE CIRCULATION. PASSENGERS AND RELATIVES OF THE EVACUEES ARE ALL GATHERED IN ONE LOCATION BEHIND A YELLOW-RIBBON LINE, LOOKING ASTONISHED TOWARD THE OPERATION.

          CARLA
          (The last evacuee arrives with his relative, running in the alley, two luggage pieces in his hand)
No, sir! You are allowed to carry only one suit.

          CITIZEN
I'm American, ma'am. Cannot have two?

                    CARLA
                    (Astonished and surprised by the question)
We announced, declared, informed, and told you, sir. It is not permitted. You are an evacuee on a military ship. This is not a commercial flight.
Register, sir, before it is too late!

                    BA
Carla, do you need any help here?
I'm done. I will join the group, and all the best.

                    CARLA
Did you finalize your wife's paper?

                    BA
Yes, yes. She is in the bus already.

                    CARLA
                    (Hugs BA)
All the best. Send us a cable after you settle in Athens.

                    BA
Sure, Carla.

EXT – SUNNY DAY – IN FRONT OF THE AMERICAN EMBASSY ON THE SEASIDE CORNICHE - BA JOINS THE EVACUEES IN THE BUS. FOLDERS IN HIS HAND. TEN JEEPS (WITH NOTATION OF PALESTINIAN LIBERATION ARMY ON THE SIDES AND PALESTINIAN FLAGS) ARRIVE WITH ARMED PERSONNEL TO SECURE THE AREA. ONE OF THE ARMED SOLDIERS JUMPS FROM THE JEEP AND GIVES INSTRUCTIONS TO THE BUS DRIVERS.

EXT - SUNNY DAY – THE CONVOY OF THREE BUSES PASSES THROUGH THE CORNICHE TOWARD RAOUCHÉ AREA FOLLOWED BY TWO JEEPS ON THE BACK OF

THE CONVOY AND ONE JEEP IN THE FRONT OF THE CONVOY.

EXT – A CONVOY OF TEN JEEPS AND SIX BUSES ARRIVE AT THE MILITARY PORT.
ARMED PERSONNEL TAKE POSITIONS AT THE SEASIDE PORT, AND THE PASSENGERS BEGIN TO LEAVE THE BUSES AND GATHER IN ONE LOCATION.
BA JOINS TWO EMBASSY PERSONNEL AT THE PORT, AND THE EVACUEES APPROACH THE EMBASSY PERSONNEL ONE BY ONE AND SHOW THEIR EVACUATION CARDS AND CONTINUE TO EMBARK IN THE US MILITARY LANDING CRAFT.

>BA

Thank you very much, Joe. Patience to you. Guard the embassy well. Hope to see you soon.
>(BA shakes the hands of two more employees on the pier and jumps inside the craft.)

EXT – AT THE PIER, US MILITARY CRAFT LEAVES THE PIER IN FRONT OF A HUGE CROWD OF PEOPLE. RELATIVES AND JOURNALISTS ON THE STREET LEVEL ARE WATCHING THE EVACUATION OF THE AMERICANS AND EMBASSY PERSONNEL.

EXT – SEAVIEW. THE CRAFT ADVANCES, AND A US MILITARY SHIP IS SEEN ON THE HORIZON.

FADE OUT:

FADE IN:

INT – INSIDE THE MILITARY SHIP. EVACUEES SALUTE THE MARINES AND OFFICERS AND SHOW THEIR

REGISTRATIONS TO THE DESK AND CLIMB TOWARD THE HIGHER FLOORS.

INT – TWO MARINES BEHIND A DESK. SURROUNDED BY TWO OFFICERS, ONE OF THEM TRIES TO READ A RED PASSPORT.

> MARINE
> (Lost and turning the pages of the red passport, right to left and left to right)

What nationality is this lady?

> MARIANNO

It is Soviet nationality, Officer.

> MARINE
> (Astonished, turns toward an officer standing beside him)

What?
Are we authorized to evacuate Soviet citizens?

> SETON
> (Consular officer interferes)

She has the clearance.
She is cleared, sir.
Her husband works for the consular section.

> MARINE
> (Relieved)

Okay! This clarifies the matter then!
Welcome on board, ma'am.
> (Stamps the evacuation card. Everybody around laughs.)

FADE OUT:

FADE IN:

EXT – NORFOLK, JOINT SPECIAL OPERATIONS COMMAND HEADQUARTERS.
RICH, DRESSED UP, WALKS TOWARD THE BUILDING.

INT – INSIDE THE BUILDING, HE CONTINUES TO WALK INSIDE ONE OF THE CORRIDORS. HE KNOCKS ON THE DOOR OF THE CHIEF OF NAVAL OPERATIONS, ENTERS THE OFFICE, AND MEETS A FEMALE OFFICER.

>   OFFICER
>   (Stands up)
> Captain Rich, they are waiting you in the conference room.
>   (She delivers a folder with TOP SECRET notation, indicating the direction of the conference room, and accompanies Rich)
>
>   RICH
> Thank you.

INT – AN OFFICER OPENS THE DOOR OF THE CONFERENCE ROOM AND INVITES RICH INSIDE.
BIG HALL, DIMLY LIGHTED AND DECORATED WITH VARIOUS FLAGS, AND THE WALLS ARE DECORATED WITH NAVY COMMANDERS' PHOTOS. SOME NAVY PHOTOS. THE CHIEF STANDS UP AND SALUTES RICH WHILE TWO PEOPLE ON THE LEFT SIDE OF THE BIG TABLE ARE SITTING.
THE CHIEF INTRODUCES RICH, AND RICH SEATS HIMSELF ON THE RIGHT SIDE OF THE TABLE, BESIDE THE CHIEF, FACING THE TWO PEOPLE.

>   CHIEF
>   (Salutes Rich and seats)
> Gentlemen, this is Commander Rich.

(Two people sitting on the left side of the table salute with their heads)

Commander, Mr. Anderson is the assistant secretary for the Foreign Operations Division.

(Rich salutes with a small movement of his head)

And Dr. Schwartz, he is from the Diplomatic Security Division of the Department of State.

(Rich, looking directly into his eyes, bows his head)

Gentlemen, we all know the purpose of our meeting here, and we would like to work together. We need Rich for a clandestine operation in Lebanon. Commander Rich will be responsible for the whole operation.

(Turning his face toward Rich)

Your mission would be to assess possible terrorist threats to American targets, survey the embassy in Beirut and marine positions, and suggest improvements.

Details of the operation are in this folder.

(Indicates the top-secret folder)

Select your team carefully, and I will be your direct contact during this operation.

MR. ANDERSON

(Looking toward Rich)

Knowing you, Commander Rich, my order to you will be "You will not fail."

RICH

(Rich rubbing the folder)

We will achieve our goal.

MR. SCHWARTZ

(Smiling to Rich)

We wish you all the luck and full support in your mission.

CHIEF
(Stands up and shakes hands with Mr. Anderson and Mr. Schwartz. Accompanies both toward the exit. Looks back and orders Rich.)
Commander, follow me to my office.

FADE OUT:

FADE IN:

INT – NORFOLK AIRPORT – AIRLINE DESK SECRETARY.

SECRETARY
(Smiles and delivers boarding pass and explains the details)
Mr. Rich, your boarding pass, Norfolk, Washington, New York.
Connection flight New York, Paris.
Overnight in Paris.
Next day, 11:30 AM, Paris. Beirut by MEA.
Have a nice trip.

RICH
(Checking around, receives his boarding pass)
Thank you.

FADE OUT:

FADE IN:

INT – PARIS ORLY AIRPORT. RICH ENTERS THE DEPARTURE SECTION AND ARRIVES AT MEA DEPARTURE DESK.

RICH
Marhaba habibi!
(Salutes in Arabic and delivers his passport and boarding pass)

COUNTER GIRL
(Smiling)
Hi! You have to say *marhaba habibti*, female of *habibi*.
(Corrects the counter girl)

RICH
See, darling. Every time, I'm mistaken. You are all *habibi*.
(Laughs with counter girl)

COUNTER GIRL
Okay. Any baggage to declare?
(She checks the reservation)

RICH
Yes. I have my carry-on baggage.
(Indicates his baggage)

COUNTER GIRL
Okay, since I'm *habibi*, I promoted your seat to first class, and these are your documents.
(Counter girl delivers boarding pass and his passports)
Bon voyage, habibi.

RICH
(Smiling to the counter girl, collects his passport and boarding pass)
Oh! Thank you. You are very kind and helpful, *habibti*.
(Both smile)

FADE OUT:

FADE IN:

INT – ARRIVAL AREA SECURITY COUNTERS AT BEIRUT INTERNATIONAL AIRPORT.
RICH FOLDS 100 LEBANESE POUNDS AND PUTS IN HIS IRISH PASSPORT AND ENTERS THE EMPTY COUNTER WHILE SMILING. HE HANDS OVER HIS PASSPORT TO A MUSTACHED IMMIGRATION OFFICER.

IMMIGRATION OFFICER CHECKS THE NAME, FOLDS THE 100-POUND BILL. AND THEN AFTER SEARCHING THE EMPTY PAGE IN THE PASSPORT, STAMPS THE PASSPORT AND RETURNS IT TO RICH.

> IMMIGRATION OFFICER
> (Smile on his face)
> *Sahafi*, journalist. *Ahlan wa Sahlan*. Welcome.

> RICH
> *Shukran.* Thank you.

EXT – OUTER DOORS OF THE AIRPORT. LOOKS LIKE A RIOT IS GOING ON. A TAXI DRIVER APPROACHES RICH WHILE A SECOND OFFERS HIS TAXI.
BOTH TAXI DRIVERS SPEAK LOUDLY AND TRY TO CONVINCE RICH TO APPROACH TOWARD THEIR TAXI.

> TAXI DRIVER
> (Opens the door on the passenger side of the taxi and tries to grab Rich's handbag. Rich refuses.)
> *Ahlan. Ahlan yaa uztez.* Welcome. Welcome, mister.
> (Gets in the car.)

> RICH
> (Rich sits on the front passenger seat.)
> *Yala habibi.* Hotel Commodore.

> TAXI DRIVER
> Yes, Hotel Commodore. You *Sahafa*?
> Me, Mohammed! call me "Abu Habib."

> RICH
> Abu Habib. Yes, *Sahafa*, you're correct.
> (Taxi driver starts his Mercedes 180 car and, while honking, advances and tries to find a way toward the main street.)

FADE OUT:

FADE IN:

EXT – LATE AFTERNOON. TAXI APPROACHES THE MAIN ENTRANCE OF HOTEL COMMODORE, HAMRA STREET, BEIRUT.
PORTMAN OPENS THE DOOR OF THE TAXI.

PASSENGER INSIDE THE TAXI STILL SPEAKS WITH THE TAXI DRIVER.

> RICH
> Yes, Abu Habib. I need a taxi, if you can. For tomorrow, not today! For the whole day.

> TAXI DRIVER
> Okay, Mr. Rich, tomorrow morning. I will wait for you here.
> (He indicates taxi stop area.)

> RICH
> How much you will charge me for the whole day?

                    TAXI DRIVER
Mr. Rich, not too much. Only 300 US dollars. I have wife and six children, you know!
          (Camera zooms to his face only.)

                    RICH
Let's agree on 200 dollars. I might need you more than one day, okay?

                    TAXI DRIVER
          (While smiling)
Okay, okay. You are a good man. I agree. Shake hands.

                    RICH
          (Shakes hand and pays taxi fare)
All right! Tomorrow morning.

EXT AND INT – RICH GETS OUT OF THE TAXI AND WALKS IN THE LOBBY TOWARD THE RECEPTION CHECK-IN DESK OF THE HOTEL COMMODORE.

                    RICH
Marhaba. I have a reservation under…
          (Submits his passport)

                    RECEPTIONIST
          (Young lady with a wide smile on her face)
Yes, Mr. Rich, journalist from Ireland. We were expecting you. One double room, B/B.
                    (She checks the list and assigns the room number. She records the data from the passport and delivers the room key.)
Room number 1236, and our welcome drinks are at the bar.
          (She indicates the in-house cocktail bar.)
Laundries will be collected from the rooms every morning before ten AM.

Diplomat, Without Portfolio

Have a nice stay.

>RICH

Thank you.
>(Grasps the room key and walks toward the bar)

FADE OUT:

FADE IN:

EXT – RICH WALKS IN THE CROWDED AND TRAFFIC-JAMMED HAMRA STREET OF BEIRUT. HE CONTINUES THROUGH RUE JEAN D'ARC STREET AND REACHES THE AUB UNIVERSITY ENTRANCE. HE STOPS, FACING THE ENTRANCE, AND CHECKS THE ENTRANCE AND EXIT OF THE STUDENTS.

HE CONTINUES WALKING AT THE SEASIDE AT THE CORNICHE, AVENUE DE PARIS. HE PASSES THE AMERICAN EMBASSY BEIRUT BUILDING AT THE SEASIDE AND CLIMBS THE STAIRWAY NEAR THE AMERICAN EMBASSY, HEADING BACK TOWARD HAMRA AND THE HOTEL COMMODORE.

FADE OUT:

FADE IN:

EXT – SUNNY MORNING, BLUE SKY. RICH WALKS TOWARD THE TAXI DRIVER WHO IS IN POSITION, WAITING FOR A CLIENT.

>TAXI DRIVER "ABU HABIB"

Good morning, Mr. Rich. *Kifak*, how are you?

> (He smiles and opens the door for Rich from the passenger side.)
>
> RICH
> (Rich gets in the taxi, and the driver gets into his seat.)

Abu Habib, good. *Kifak?*
Today, you are going to take me to the museum area and then Corniche and then Raouché Corniche, and we'll end up with Manara Corniche.

> TAXI DRIVER "ABU HABIB"
> (Thinks a little bit while his eyes are blinking.)

Mr. Rich, Corniche Raouché and Manara are okay. But museum area, it's not okay. Danger area.
I will call friend. If he says okay, I will go for you to museum area.

EXT – SUNNY MORNING. TAXI SCROLLING IN THE TRAFFIC-JAMMED STREETS OF BEIRUT WHILE "ABU HABIB" INDICATES VARIOUS BUILDINGS FROM HAMRA STREET TO THE SEASIDE.
BUILDINGS OCCUPIED BY "SYRIAN ARMY PERSONNEL" AND VARIOUS LOCAL WEST BEIRUT MILITIAS "MOURABITOUN," "SYRIAN POPULAR FRONT," AND "AMAL."

> TAXI DRIVER "ABU HABIB"
> (Abu Habib stops his car in front of a coffee shop and speaks to Rich.)

Mr. Rich, this is coffee shop of my cousin. I will call a friend, and I will take you also to the museum area, okay?

> RICH
> (Looking toward "Abu Habib")

You are the boss. You know better.

TAXI DRIVER "ABU HABIB"
(Enters the coffee shop while Rich waits in the taxi. After a while, he returns, smiling.)
Okay, Mr. Rich, we go. But we will not stay long. We turn quickly.

EXT – "ABU HABIB" REACHES THE MUSEUM AREA TO A MILITARY ROADBLOCK, WITH SYRIAN ARMY CONTROLLING THE TRAFFIC BETWEEN EAST AND WEST BEIRUT. HE STOPS HIS TAXI AT THE ROADBLOCK.

TAXI DRIVER "ABU HABIB"
(Salutes the Syrian Army soldiers at the roadblock.)
Marhaba ya Shabab!
(Hi guys.)

SOLDIER
(Speaks Arabic) Where are you heading?

TAXI DRIVER "ABU HABIB"
(Speaks Arabic) We will turn from here.
(Indicating the nearby area)

SOLDIER
(Speaking Arabic) Who is this man with you?

TAXI DRIVER "ABU HABIB"
(Speaking Arabic) Sahafe from Irlanda.

SOLDIER
(Speaking Arabic) Okay. Go and return.

EXT – "ABU HABIB" ADVANCES THIRTY TO FORTY FEET AND RETURNS TOWARD WEST BEIRUT WHILE SALUTING TO THE SOLDIERS.

TAXI DRIVER "ABU HABIB"
See, Mr. Rich? It is dangerous the other side.
   (Indicates the East Beirut Christian side.)
But for you, I come.

RICH
(Tries to check all the area while answering "Abu Habib" the driver.)
Now I understand you, Abu Habib.

TAXI DRIVER "ABU HABIB"
Yes, yes! Dangerous.
Now I will take you to the Corniche, Ain el-Mreisseh, American embassy, and then coffee shop and fish restaurant at the seaside.

EXT –INT TAXI STOPS AT SEASIDE COFFEE SHOP, AND "ABU HABIB" AND RICH ENTER THE COFFEE SHOP AND SIT AROUND A SMALL ROUND TABLE.
ABU HABIB ORDERS TWO COFFEES WITH TWO GLASSES OF WATER.

RICH
(Drinking the coffee)
Abu Habib, I have to rent an office and an apartment nearby this area. It must be good. You know I cannot stay long period in the hotel.

TAXI DRIVER "ABU HABIB"
(Excited)
Yes, Mr. Rich. I will help you. I have a cousin who knows a lot of places in this area, sea view and good apartments.

RICH
(Camera showing only his face.)

Diplomat, Without Portfolio

Okay. Then, as of tomorrow, we will look to rent apartments too before my employees reaching Beirut.

        TAXI DRIVER "ABU HABIB"
I will call tonight, get addresses, and tomorrow, we will go together and see the apartments. Okay?

FADE OUT:

FADE IN:

INT – RICH ENTERS THE LOBBY OF HOTEL COMMODORE AND GETS THE ELEVATOR TOWARD HIS ROOM.
RICH CHECKS HIS STUFF IN HIS CARRY-ON BAG AND HANDBAG AND BEGINS TO LAUGH.

(SHAKES HIS HEAD WHILE CHECKING HIS BAG)

        RICH
Welcome to ME. Welcome to Lebanon!
You think I don't know?
Good! Nothing is missing!

FADE OUT:

FADE IN:

INT – DAYLIGHT - LONDON AIRPORT CHECK-IN DESK – FOUR PEOPLE LINE UP AND COMPLETE THEIR CHECK-IN TO THE FLIGHT LONDON/PARIS/FRANKFURT TO DAMASCUS.

INT – DAYLIGHT - AMSTERDAM AIRPORT CHECK-IN DESK – FOUR PEOPLE LINE UP AND COMPLETE THEIR

CHECK-IN TO THE FLIGHT AMSTERDAM/ATHENS/ LARNACA.

EXT – LATE EVENING, LARNACA PORT - GROUP OF FOUR WHO FLEW FROM AMSTERDAM LINE UP TO GET THE FERRYBOAT FROM LARNACA TO JOUNIEH PORT, BEIRUT.

FADE OUT:

FADE IN:

EXT – SIGONELLA AIRBASE IN SICILY – COMMANDER INSTRUCTS THE PILOT TO CARRY FOUR OFFICERS AND INDICATES AIR SHUTTLE, NAVY C-2 (GREYHOUND COD – CARRIER ONBOARD DELIVERY).
HEAVY HELICOPTER SOUND IN THE BACKSTAGE SCENE AND TWO PEOPLE HELPING THE CREW, PREPARATION FOR THE FLIGHT.

    COMMANDER
    (Only radio message at the background, to pilot)
This is Commander Norman.
Pilot, drop the group into the flight deck of USS *Independence*, just off the Lebanese Coast.
Roger.

    PILOT
    (Only radio message at the background, to commander)
Yes, sir!

EXT - FLIGHT MONITOR, SIGNALS FOUR PEOPLE TO JUMP ON C-2 HELICOPTER. THEY CARRY WITH THEM VARIOUS BOXES AND HEAVY BAGS AND JUMP TO THE HELICOPTER.

HELICOPTER SLOWLY MOVES AND CLIMBS HEIGHT AND DISAPPEARS IN THE DARK.

FADE OUT:

FADE IN:

EXT – DARK SKY, FOUR MARINES ON USS *INDEPENDENCE*. A BIG DINGHY READY TO BE DROPPED TO THE SEA. A PILE OF MILITARY EQUIPMENT AND BAGS AND BOXES BEHIND THE SCENE.

>   COMMANDER
>   (Instructs two separate marine contingents)
>   Drop them to the shore after changing their clothing.

>   MARINE

Yes, sir.

EXT- DARK SKY, FOUR PEOPLE DRESSED AS MARINES CARRY ALL THE EQUIPMENT, BOXES, AND BAGS TO THE DINGHY IN THE SEA. THE DINGHY MOVES IN THE DARK TOWARD THE SHORE ALONG WITH SIX SEPARATE MARINE CONTINGENTS. THE SCENE FADES ON THE BACKGROUND – USS *INDEPENDENCE*, WHILE DINGHY LEAVES THE WARSHIP.

FADE OUT:

FADE IN:

EXT- SEASHORE OF BAY JOUNIEH, EARLY HOURS OF THE MORNING. A GROUP OF MARINES PULL THE DINGHY TOWARD THE SHORE. FOUR ARMED MILITIA MEMBERS

AT THE SHORE, WITH THEIR SEDAN JEEP-TYPE CARS, GIVE A HAND TO THE ARRIVING MARINES.
THE SIX MARINES CHANGE THEIR MILITARY CLOTHING AND THROW THEM IN THE DINGHY.
THE OTHER FOUR MARINES EMPTY EQUIPMENT, BOXES, AND AMMUNITION FROM THE DINGHY AND PUT THEM IN THREE JEEPS, WHICH ARE ON THE SHORE.

           MILITIA LEADER
           (Radio equipment in his hand, salutes the group leader)
Welcome, Captain!
           (Militia leader murmurs words to the ear of the group leader and orders his men on the shore to give a hand to the marines.)
Everything is in order, and we will take you to the destination.

           GROUP LEADER
All right!
           (Carefully controls the militiamen and gives his order by his hand to deliver the equipment, boxes, and bags to the jeeps.)

           MARINE
           (With the remaining three marines in the dinghy, he starts the dinghy. And after saluting the group leader, he advances toward the sea.)
Guys! Keep your heads down!

           GROUP LEADER
           (Saluting the marine)
Yes, sir! See you soon.

EXT – STILL DARK AND VIOLET SKY. THE SIX NEWLY ARRIVED MARINES AND FOUR ARMED MILITIAS LEAVE

Diplomat, Without Portfolio

THE SHORE WITH THREE SEDAN JEEPS, HEADING TOWARD JOUNIEH CITY.

FADE OUT:

FADE IN:

EXT – SUNNY MIDDAY, NEAR THE MUSEUM CROSSING AREA. RICH, DRESSED LIKE A LOCAL COUNTRYMAN, WAITS WHILE LEANING AGAINST THE WALL.
THREE SEDAN JEEPS APPROACH HIS LOCATION, AND ALL PARK BEHIND EACH OTHER.
RICH, NOTICING DENISE (GROUP LEADER), RAISES HIS THUMB UP WHILE THE FOURTH SEDAN APPROACHES, PARKS, AND JOINS THE THREE SEDANS.
RICH JOINS THE FIRST SEDAN, AND THE CONVOY OF THE FIRST TWO SEDANS LEAVE FOR WEST BEIRUT.
AFTER A SMALL INTERRUPTION, THE REMAINING TWO SEDANS HEAD TOWARD WEST BEIRUT.

FADE OUT:

FADE IN:

INT – SIX PEOPLE IN A ROOM, WORKING ON DIFFERENT TYPEWRITERS. ON THE WALLS, A POSTER OF CASTRO GIVING A SPEECH. ON THE SECOND WALL, A CALENDAR, AND BESIDE THE CALENDAR WHITEBOARD, NOTES OF SPEECH AT 11:00 GMT.
ON THE THIRD WALL IS LOCAL HEAD OF LEBANESE SOCIAL PARTY LEADER JUMBLATT'S POSTER.
TWO PEOPLE ARE READING MAGAZINES AND ASKING RICH QUESTIONS.

>   RICH
>   (Handing some papers to Peter)
>   Are you and your team ready for tonight?
>
>   PETER
>   Yes, Rich, with all the details.
>
>   RICH
>   (Looking with satisfied appearance)
>   Good. Will be waiting for midnight dinner.

THE SOUND OF A HUGE EXPLOSION OUTSIDE THE OFFICE HALTS THE CONVERSATION IN THE ROOM.

>   PETER
>   Rich, this is the second week in Beirut. I counted. We'd heard half a dozen car bombs go off.
>
>   RICH
>   We heard too, and good that you counted them. How about the building?
>
>   PETER
>   No doubt, this building is watched by different people. We don't know them, but obvious that it is under surveillance every moment by many groups.

EXT – DARK STREETS FOUR PEOPLE WEARING VERY CASUAL DRESSES WALKING IN THE STREET—TWO ON ONE SIDE AND TWO ON THE OTHER SIDE OF THE STREET.
ONE PASSES IN FRONT OF A HUGE BUILDING, AND THE REMAINING THREE CONTINUE THEIR WALKING. ONE OF THEM IS HOLDING A TRIPOD IN HIS HAND, AND A CAMERA HANGS FROM HIS SHOULDER.

ONE PERSON STANDS ON THE CORNER OF THE BUILDING, JUST LOOKING AROUND. AND HE PULLS A FLAT CARTON AND CONVERTS IT TO A BOX AND LEAVES IT ON THE CORNER WHERE HE IS STANDING.
HE WAITS TWENTY SECONDS AND RETURNS AND WALKS VERY SLOWLY, LOOKING HERE AND THERE, AND CROSSES THE STREET FROM THE ALLEY OF THE HUGE SEVEN-FLOOR BUILDING.
ONE GUY PULLS THE TUBE, WHICH IS WRAPPED TO THE TRIPOD, AND ALONG WITH THE SECOND GUY, INSTALLS THE TUBE—BOTH ENDS CLOSED—EXACTLY FACING THE SAME BUILDING WHERE ONE OF THE GUYS LEFT THE BOX IN ITS CORNER. HE WRAPS THE TUBE TO THE SEASIDE POLE, AND THE OTHER TWO CONTROLS WHILE THE FOURTH LOOKS AROUND TO CHECK BUT NOTICES NO ONE.
AND HE WALKS VERY STEADY AND FOLLOWS FIVE YARDS BEHIND THEM.

FADE OUT:

FADE IN:

INT- A LIGHTED ROOM WHERE THREE GUYS ARE READING, AND ONE OF THEM IS TYPING ON A TYPEWRITER. RICH IS IN A HIDDEN CORNER OF THE ROOM, TALKING ON A RADIO WITH SOME PAPERS IN HIS HAND.

        RICH
Yes, sir. Midnight dinner is over, and guys are at home.
    (Interruption)
All right, sir. Over.
    (Rich leaves the room and appears in a different room and distributes some printed materials and

>   asks Peter to distribute other bunches at every corner
>   of the house, to make it look messy.)
> Peter tries to distribute them here and there.
>   (He applauds once)
>   Guys, let's go over our plans for tomorrow.

FADE OUT:

FADE IN:

EXT – (RICH AND PETER) TOGETHER WALKING IN SPEARS STREET AND TAKING SOME PHOTOS OF BUILDINGS, RESTAURANTS, AND A CHICKEN SANDWICH RESTAURANT.

>   PETER
>   (Camera toward Rich)
>   Rich, say "I love you, ma'am."
>
>   RICH
>   (Laughs and indicates with his eye the nearby
>   building with flags on the balcony)

PETER ACTS LIKE A JOURNALIST AND INTERVIEWS AN OLD MAN WHO IS HAPPILY EXPLAINING TO PETER AND LAUGHING WITH HIM AT HIS STATEMENTS.

FOUR TEENAGERS, TWO WITH DRAWN PISTOLS AND TWO WITH AK-47s (ARMED MILITIA MEMBERS), WHILE WALKING IN THE STREET, NOTICE PETER TAKING PHOTOS OF THE SHOPS AND BUILDINGS.

>   FIRST MILITIA – YOUNG MAN
>   (Rushing toward Peter. Signals to stop.)
>   Hey! Hey! No photos.

PETER
Sahafa. Sahafa, boys. We are *sahafa.*
>(Journalist, journalist, we are journalists.)

RICH
>(Noticing the guys, tries to stop them by raising his arms up and puts his back against the wall while smiling)

What's up?
Vous parlez francais?

SECOND MILITIA
>(In heavy French)

(Quesque vous faite ici?)
What are you doing here?

RICH
Je suis journaliste. Sahafa, press.
(I'm Journalist, journalist.)

SECOND MILITIA
>(Turns to his friends and translates in Arabic)

Your friend took a photo of this place. Secret military place.
>(Indicating a building)

This is Mourabitoun center.

RICH
>(Turns towards Peter- - and shouts "be ashamed")

Don't you see this is militia center?
>(Peter hangs his head and, ashamed, opens the back of the camera. He pulls the film out, exposing the entire roll.)

Ask them. Is it okay now?
>(Continues Rich)

SECOND MILITIA
(He takes the film)
Militia live here. That's a secret installation.
(He nods seriously.)

RICH
And the next street there?
(He points west)

SECOND MILITIA
(He shakes his head)
Belongs to Amal—Shia militia.

RICH
(He indicates eastward)
And there?

SECOND MILITIA
One street, Mourabitoun. Next street, Syrian National Party.
(He points beyond Hamra Street)
There Hezbollah.

RICH
(Inclines his head graciously)
Shukran, Merci beaucoup!
We will be cautious and will not take pictures. Thank you.
(Rich shakes the hand of the teenager and salutes the others.)

RICH AND PETER: THEY RUSH TOWARD THE SANDWICH SHOP TO SECURE THEIR SANDWICHES AND AVOID THE INTEREST OF MILITIAMEN AND THE CROWD AROUND THEM.

FADE IN:

INT - CHRISTMAS EVE 1982. A GROUP OF SIX PEOPLE SITTING IN A BIG BALCONY FACING THE SEA VIEW AND DINING ON CHICKEN SANDWICHES, FRENCH FRIES, AND SOME COKE BOTTLES HERE AND THERE ON THE TABLE.

>   (RICH)
>   (Bites his sandwich)
> They will hit the embassy with RPGs.

>   (PETER)
> If you gonna hit an embassy, you want to hit it hard.

>   (RICH)
> Hezbollah's got tanks too.
> Phalangists probably have as much armor as the Lebanese Army too.

>   (PETER)
> This place is a frigging cardboard building.
> We left the box, and no one pulled it for thirty-six hours.
> The tube is still in its place, and no one noticed that it is aimed towards the ambassador's floor.

>   RICH
> Well, he's right.
> Nothing except radio-controlled car bomb is what they'll use.
> We drove along Corniche al-Mazraa, Fakahani, the district in which the PLO had its offices during its long occupation of Lebanon.
> Bir Hassan and Bir Abed, two of the poorer Shia neighborhoods.
> It seems likely places for bomb makers to live in.

> PETER
> (Looking worried)

So let's do some reverse engineering. Radio-controlled bombs are detonated by sending a signal over a thousand-foot range frequency.

If you broadcast the range of frequencies used by radio-control devices and you hit an active one, the detonator will activate, and the bomb will go off.

> RICH
> (Looks satisfied and ready to act)

I will request a meeting with senior officials at the embassy after forty-eight hours.

We will report our final findings and suggestions.

Me and Peter would show up, and we will change our appearance just in case the watchers are sniffing around the comings and goings.

FADE OUT:

FADE IN:

INT – HIGHLY DECORATED RECEPTION ROOM WITH VARIOUS CORNERS AND BIG COUCHES. RICH AND PETER ARE SITTING IN THEIR CASUAL CLOTHING.

A TALL DISTINGUISHED-LOOKING GRAY-HAIRED DIPLOMAT AND AN AIDE ENTER THE ROOM.

> (DIPLOMAT)
> (Cold, unwillingly shakes hands)

Gentlemen, good morning.

Diplomat, Without Portfolio

(RICH)
(Stands up and shakes hands first with the diplomat and then his aide. Peter follows the same.)
Good morning, sir.
I'm Rich. And this is Peter, my aide. We are on special mission in Beirut to ascertain possible terrorist threats to American targets.

(DIPLOMAT)
(With open eyes)
Are you two alone here?

(RICH)
No, sir. Our other experts and aides are on their missions and await my instructions—

(DIPLOMAT)
(Responds without waiting for an explanation)
And what's going to be that instruction?

(RICH)
Sir, after thorough investigations and three weeks of surveying the embassy site, your security apparatus has gaping holes. We have enough evidence and believe you're easily vulnerable to attack at any moment by any armed groupings.

(DIPLOMAT)
(Looks annoyed and looks at his aide. He clears his throat.)

Commander, this mission has managed to withstand the Lebanese civil war, which has gone on unabated since 1975. We have endured the PLO, the Syrians, and the Israelis.

RICH
But the situation has changed in the past few weeks, sir.

Maronites claim that Americans are seen as allies and—

(DIPLOMAT)
(He cuts Rich off)
I'm well aware, Commander, of the political situation here. And while there is some flux in the situation, our security posture has no need of change.
Let me remind you, Commander, that I know this country and these people. And I know and trust my staff.
The security of this embassy is airtight.
That is my position.

(RICH)
(Looking directly into the diplomat's eyes)
With all respect, sir. I think your situation is about to become all fluxed up.

(DIPLOMAT)
(Flushed)
Commander, there's no need.

(RICH)
Our survey indicates a strong possibility that the embassy will be the focus of a car-bomb attack in the near future.
Therefore, I strongly recommend, sir, that you reconfigure the access to the embassy, bolster the armed presence on your perimeters, and employ devices such as these.
(Rich indicates a box)
It's a radio transmitter that broadcasts the frequencies commonly used to detonate car bombs.
It has a range of about one thousand feet.

(Cont.)
gest that you set a pair of these on the roof. That way, dio-controlled car bombs in the vicinity will detonate they get close enough to do any damage to the embassy.

(DIPLOMAT)
(Looking at his aide and then at Rich)
You mean, we'd destroy the car bomb before it got to the embassy?

(RICH)
Yes, sir!

(DIPLOMAT)
(Annoyed)
But that would cause casualties.

(RICH)
Well, yes, sir. But—

(DIPLOMAT)
(Moving in his chair)
That is unacceptable.

(RICH)
What is?

(DIPLOMAT)
(Annoyed, the dissatisfaction is clear on his face)
Causing casualties. We can't cause casualties. Indiscriminate casualties would be bad for our diplomatic image.

(RICH)
(Furious as Peter is collecting the stuff from the table)
We're talking about keeping you and your people alive, sir.

(DIPLOMAT)
Not like that.

                    (SENIOR AIDE)
                (Looking at the black box distastefully.)
          Such things aren't...correct!

                    (DIPLOMAT)
          That's not a proper way to do business, Commander.
          Such devices would be unfair to the Lebanese population,
          and I refuse to have anything to do with them.
                    (He stands up.)
          Now if you'll excuse me.
          Thank you for coming, Commander.
          I hope you and your men have a safe journey back home.

FADE OUT:

FADE IN:

EXT – DARK MIDNIGHT ON THE BEACH, BACKGROUND CITY LIGHTS OF JOUNIEH BAY IN A DISTANCE HORIZON. A GROUP OF TWELVE PEOPLE MANAGE TO EMPTY BAGS, BOXES, AND DEVICES FROM THREE STATION WAGONS. A COUPLE OF LOCAL MILITIA MEMBERS HELP THE GROUP TO EMPTY THE VANS.

                    RICH
                (Flashes his navy ID toward the sea)
          They are near, guys. Be prepared.

EXT – DARK NIGHT - SIX MEN WITH MILITARY CLOTHING CONTINUE TO EMPTY BAGS AND SOME BOXES FROM THREE VANS AND INSERT THEM IN A BIG DINGHY. RICH SALUTES A MAN WITH A MILITARY HAT.

                    RICH
          Commander, thank you for your support.

Diplomat, Without Portfolio

> COMMANDER
> Welcome, Rich. Safe trip.

THE BIG DINGHY FERRIES TOWARD THE MIDDLE OF THE SEA.

FADE OUT:

FADE IN:

EXT – DARK EVENING – NEIGHBOR FACING BA'S APARTMENT SHOUTING LOUDLY.

INT - BA IS SEATED WITH HIS FAMILY MEMBERS, EATING SNACKS AND DRINKING SOFT DRINKS.

> NEIGHBOR
> (Sounding high and shouting)
> BA! BA! Hey, BA!

> BA
> (Jumps from his seat and goes out toward the balcony)
> This is our neighbor from the facing balcony. What does he want?
> Hey, Mayor! What's going on?

EXT – IN THE DARK

> NEIGHBOR
> (Shouts from balcony, from the opposite building)
> I think it's an overseas call.
> An American wants to talk to you. Come over and answer the phone.

> BA
> All right, Mayor. Hold the line. I'll be there.

INT – BA LEAVES HIS APARTMENT AND GOES TO ANSWER THE PHONE IN THE OPPOSITE APARTMENT.

INT – REACHES TO THE PHONE AND SPEAKS ON THE PHONE.

> BA
> Yes, who's this?

> (Sound from the Other Side)
> Hey, Bedros! This is Jim from the embassy.
> Sorry, I'm calling you through your neighbor's phone.
> I'm lucky to catch his line.
> I know all the phone lines are unreachable.

> BA
> Hi, Jim. Yes, I know. After the invasion, now everything is in jeopardy.
> Electricity, phones, TV…

> (Sound from the Other side)
> I understand. It seems this will continue for a while.
> I have instructions to see you.
> Maybe in a remote and safer place.
> How about Jounieh?
> Maybe the Corner Café, tomorrow morning.

> BA
> Okay. I know where it is.
> I will be there nine o'clock.
> How about that?

> (Sound from the Other side)
> Sounds good. I'll be there.
> BA, do you have any access with one of our drivers?
> I have an embassy car available with me.
> He will be a good help.

> BA
> Don't worry. I will locate one and bring him with me.
> Okay. See you tomorrow at nine.

> (Sound from the Other side)
> Perfect! Will see you at nine.

INT – BA ENDS HIS CONVERSATION AND CHATS WITH THE MAYOR.

> BA
> Thank you, Mayor.
> (Looks at his watch)
> Ten PM now. And good that I had given your phone number also to my colleagues.
> I have to report to duty tomorrow morning.
> He was the press attaché of the embassy.

> MAYOR – NEIGHBOR
> No problem, BA. Anytime.
> With this situation—occupied by Syrians, Israelis, Palestinians—it is not known where we are heading.
> At least, after months of unemployment, you report to duty.

> BA
> Yes! Paid unemployment.
> Embassy is closed, and we are sitting at home and doing nothing. It's annoying, Mayor.
> (BA looks at his watch again and continues.)
> I'm going to use the phone one more time, Mayor. Can I?

MAYOR – NEIGHBOR

BA, come on! You don't need permission.
Finalize your work.

BA
(Calls the numbers on the phone)
Sako! Is that you?
You are not at sleep?

(Sound from the Other Side)
Nooo. Not yet, BA!

BA
What are you doing?

(Sound from the Other Side)
I'm drinking my whisky, my friend.
No embassy, no work.

BA
Don't drink too much, Sako! Sleep early.
They called me from the embassy.
I'm going to pick you up tomorrow morning and will take you with me to Jounieh.

(Sound from the Other Side)
Even if I drink the whole bottle—ready anytime, BA.
You know me.

BA
All right, all right.
Be ready eight am. I will come and pick you.
Okay! It will take an hour to reach to Jounieh.
Say hello to your wife and kids.
See you!

FADE OUT:

FADE IN:

INT – DIM LIGHTING IN A ROOM – BA, AT HIS APARTMENT, TALKS WITH HIS WIFE AND CHILDREN.

>BA
>It was Jim from the embassy.
>I have to see him in Jounieh tomorrow morning and discuss various issues.
>Embassy relocation, consulate, personnel, and so on.

INT – CHILDREN STOP THEIR READING AND BOTH STARE AND LISTEN TO BA'S CONVERSATION.

>MARIANNO
>(Stops her knitting work)
>Good! Good news. At least, you will be busy.

>BA
>Yes, Marianno. Also, I will bring Sako with me. We are in need of his services.
>I will not be alone in this unsafe and undetermined situation. At least, I'm going back and forth with him.

FADE OUT:

FADE IN:

EXT – IN THE FRONT OF "CORNER" SEASIDE CAFÉ, OPEN PARKING LOT SPACE, ON THE TRUNK OF AN OFFICIAL CAR, BA IS TYPING. JIM—IN CASUAL SHIRT AND PANTS—TALKS WITH SEVEN TO EIGHT PEOPLE AROUND HIM.

SAKO IS HOLDING A WIRELESS PHONE BOX IN HIS
HAND, DIALING ON THE PHONE.

> BA
> Jim, these recommendation letters are ready, along with their
> US passports. Have to contact Joe Attik's office, Port Jounieh.

> JIM
> Good, BA. I will call him now, and we have to see him face
> to face.
> We have already fifteen US citizens, if he wants to operate his
> yacht to Larnaca.

> BA
> Okay. I will ask Sako to contact him, and we go and see him.
> How about the exit and passage permits from Lebanese and
> Israeli authorities?

> JIM
> I will manage that with the ambassador and secure the
> passage, but they must have these recommendations in their
> hands.

FADE OUT:

FADE IN:

EXT - PORT JOUNIEH, NOONTIME. BA AND JIM REACH IN FRONT OF AN OFFICE. TWO FORTY-INCH CONTAINERS HAVE BEEN CONVERTED INTO OFFICES WITH THREE SMALL DESKS. EMPLOYEES ARE TYPING AND WORKING. THE OFFICE IS EQUIPPED WITH A WIRELESS COMMUNICATION SYSTEM AND A BIG TV SET, AND TWO FEMALE EMPLOYEES ARE TYPING.

INT – SAKO PARKS THE CAR IN FRONT OF THE OFFICE.
BA AND JIM ENTER THE OFFICE. SAKO WAITS OUTSIDE.

> BA
>
> *Ahlan*, Joe. How are you?

> JOE
>
> BA, *kifak*! You were supposed to come early.

> BA
>
> You're right, but we are busy just issuing recommendation letters to our citizens so that they can secure a safe passage. Hey, Joe. This is Mr. Jim, the press attaché of the embassy. We would like to talk to you about a very official matter.

> JOE
>
> Welcome, Jim!
> Have you been in Jounieh?

> JIM
>
> This is my first visit, thanks to BA and Sako. I'm here so that we can discuss and prepare a secured link between Jounieh and Larnaca.

> JOE
>
> All right, all right.
> Please come into my office, and we will talk.

INT – BA FOLLOWS JOE, AND JIM FOLLOWS THE GROUP. THEY ALL SIT IN A ROOM SEPARATED BY A GLASS PARTITION.

> BA
>
> Joe, we need your help and advice so that we can operate this link.

We know that you can manage some yachts, and we need a regular liner.

JIM
Oh yes, Joe!
We rely on you and will benefit from your expertise. And as you know, yachts have to be reliable and secured.
We don't want any troubles or problems in the middle of the Mediterranean.

JOE
Okay. I understand.
(He thinks a little bit and continues)
I will secure you the best yachts!
But the problem is that you have to secure the passage through the office of our friends, Lebanese forces. And then my brother, the Israelis, are a big problem.
They are very tough!
They don't want us to release any yacht from Port Jounieh, except some foodstuff cargo boats.

JIM
Joe, if you supply us the yachts, I promise to help you and try to get all the permissions from the Lebanese forces and the Israelis through our ambassador.
The ambassador wants secure passage of our citizens from Port Jounieh.
They cannot travel through Beirut Airport. They are stuck in East Beirut.

JOE
(Speaks in Arabic to BA)
BA, my friend, this is a business, and I have to work.
I have to locate the best yachts.

> BA
> (Explains to Jim while addressing Joe)
> We understand, Joe!
> We know that you have to make money from this business, but we are responsible in front of the embassy and the ambassador.
> Choose the yachts, and we will report to the ambassador. And please do your best and as soon as possible.

> JOE
> Okay. I will.

> JIM
> Thank you. *Shukran ya habibi.*
> (Thank you, my friend.)
> Will contact you after tomorrow.

INT/EXT – BA AND JIM LEAVE THE OFFICE, AND SAKO OPENS THE DOOR OF THE CAR FOR THEM. BA AND JIM SIT AT THE BACK SEAT OF THE CAR AND LEAVE TOGETHER.

EXT – INSIDE THE CAR - JIM AND BA, SEATED IN THE CAR, DISCUSS THE RESULT OF THE CONVERSATION WITH JOE.

> JIM
> Good, BA! This was the first step and a good choice if we manage to arrange this link. The ambassador will be very happy.

> BA
> Yes, Jim. I'm sure Joe will manage this and hope we will be able to open the link from the Port Jounieh.

EXT – A CONVOY OF ISRAELI JEEPS AND TWO ARMED VEHICLES PASS FROM THE OTHER DIRECTION OF THE STREET.

>JIM
>Oh my god. Good. They did not notice that we are from the US diplomatic mission.

>BA
>No, they are not in need of US visas. They are vacationing, and they are in need of Palestinians in Jounieh.
>(Jim and BA smile and stare at the convoy)

FADE OUT:

FADE IN:

EXT - BA, ALONG WITH AN EMPLOYEE INSIDE AN AMERICAN CAR, ARRIVE IN FRONT OF AN OLD GOVERNMENT BUILDING.

DRIVER DROPS BA AND THE EMPLOYEE AT THE FRONT GATE OF THE GOVERNMENT BUILDING. THERE IS A LEBANESE FLAG ON THE BUILDING.

INT – BA AND THE EMPLOYEE WALK IN THE HALL OF THE BUILDING AND ENTER A BIG HIGH-CEILINGED ROOM.

>BA
>(With a big smile on his face)
>Chief! Good morning.
>This is Mr. Jim from the embassy, the press attaché.

CHIEF MUNICIPALITY
Ahlan! BA, welcome to the municipality of Jounieh.
It's been a long time.
How are you?
Welcome, Mr. Jim. What a surprise to me.

JIM
Thank you, Chief. Nice meeting you.
Nice building.
BA speaks highly about you, and he says you still keep your friendship with our embassy personnel.

BA
You have kind regards from our mutual friend, Monic.
She is in Athens. She says hi to you.

CHIEF MUNICIPALITY
Yes, thank you!
How is she doing?
I really miss her.
Nice lady. She loved Lebanon.

INT – EMPLOYEE ENTERS THE ROOM AND STANDS NEAR THE CHIEF'S DESK.

EMPLOYEE OF MUNICIPALITY
What would you like to drink—coffee, tea, lemonade?

BA
Coffee please. Thank you.

JIM
Same please. Thanks.

CHIEF MUNICIPALITY
Ahlan Oua Sahlan, BA and Mr. Jim.
What can I do for you?

BA
Chief, we are here with my colleague Jim to request from you a big favor.

CHIEF MUNICIPALITY
Walaw! Anything for you!
You are our friend, and we have to help you.

BA
Chief, as you know, after the Israeli invasion, we were obliged to terminate our operations at the embassy building in East Beirut.
Today, there is no single operation at all in that building.
We are here with my colleague, Jim, to ask you for your help, if you can accommodate us with an office here in the Municipality building.
We would like do some consular work for our American citizens.

INT – AN EMPLOYEE ENTERS THE ROOM AND BRINGS TWO CUPS OF COFFEE AND A GLASS OF JUS. HE PUTS THE JUS ON THE CHIEF'S DESK AND THE TWO COFFEE CUPS ON A SMALL TABLE IN FRONT OF BA AND JIM.

CHIEF MUNICIPALITY
       (Smiling and relieved)
Walaw! You requested and are in need of a room.
I'm going to give you a big hall instead of a room.
Our second floor is empty and has all the necessary furniture, and it is under your disposition as of this moment. It can accommodate even all your employees.

> JIM
> (Astonished)
> Perfect, Chief!

> BA
> Thank you, Chief!
> (BA stands up and shakes the chief's hand)
> You are always helpful.
> (Gets the coffee cup and begins to drink the coffee. Jim repeats the same.)

> CHIEF MUNICIPALITY
> Jim, BA, I repeat, you can begin as of today. The hall is available, and it's under your—

> BA
> Chief, as of tomorrow, Jim and me will meet upstairs and will announce through media about our limited services at the Municipality building.

> CHIEF MUNICIPALITY
> Of course, with all our blessings.

Ext - JIM AND BA AT THE ENTRANCE OF THE BUILDING. THEY SAY FAREWELL TO THE CHIEF AND SHAKE HANDS WITH HIM.

EXT – SAKO RUSHES TO OPEN THE CAR DOOR FOR JIM AND BA. BOTH SIT AT THE REAR OF THE CAR, AND THEY CHAT.

> JIM
> Very polite and handsome person.
> Very nice, very fruitful day.
> Thank you, BA.

Now I know why the ambassador and your friend Linda had given your name to me!
Through your contacts and efforts today, we are destined for success.

BA
Yes, Jim. We kept our relationship with our friends on a very high level, and here we go.
Another fruitful result.
Jim, you have to inform the big boss.

JIM
Oh yes! We will stop in a remote area and use this big phone, and I have to report about all our activity.
I will mention to Mr. Ambassador your input, BA, arranging all these meetings.

BA
Oh yes. Thank you! Mission accomplished.

FADE OUT:

FADE IN:

INT – IN A LONG HALL AROUND TWO BIG TABLES, JIM IS TYPING LETTERS AND DISCUSSING TRAVEL ISSUES WITH VARIOUS PEOPLE.

SARKIS IS SMOKING AND, FROM TIME TO TIME, MANAGING TO LOCATE SEATS FOR THE NEWCOMERS TO THE HALL.

BA IS EXPLAINING AND GIVING DETAILS TO THE BBC, REUTERS, AND LOCAL NEWSPAPER JOURNALISTS

ABOUT THE LIMITED CONSULAR OPERATION IN THE LOCALITY.

> BA
> Yes, it's only for US citizens.
> It's going to be like chartered boats, from Port Jounieh to Larnaca.

> BBC/TV CORRESPONDENT
> Are you planning any evacuation of US citizens and foreign nationals?

> BA
> No, no, no! We know nothing yet about any possible evacuation.
> This is just securing the passage of our US citizens outside of Beirut.

> REUTERS CORRESPONDENT
> Are you issuing any special permits for them?

> BA
> Yes, to our citizens only.
> We are issuing a recommendation letter so that they have secured exit passage from Lebanese authorities and exit from Port Jounieh, at the same time, from the Israelis in the middle of the Mediterranean.

> VOL CORRESPONDENT
> Do you plan to issue US visas here?

> BA
> We have no instructions now to issue US visas.
> We are handling only US Interest Section here.
> If the situation remains as it is, we might begin in visa procedures!

                    BA
Thank you, guys. I have no further information at this time.
If you'll excuse me, I have to help my colleague.

INT – BA LEAVES THE MEDIA PEOPLE AND JOINS JIM TO HELP HIM IN HIS WORK.

                    BA
              (Murmurs to Jim)
I have good news, Jim.
Joe managed to locate a yacht.
His first yacht will be ready after tomorrow.
We can accommodate up to twenty.

                    JIM
              (Murmurs to BA)
Good!
We have already issued fifteen recommendation letters, so I'm sure, up to tomorrow, we will add five more for him.
So our door opened to the outside world, BA!

                    BA
Yes, Jim. With this yacht, we will be the first to initiate this link.

                    JIM
Then let me inform the ambassador.
He will be delighted with this news.

INT – JIM WALKS TO THE OTHER END OF THE HALL TO USE THE WIRELESS PHONE LOCATED ON A SPECIAL TABLE.

FADE OUT:

FADE IN:

EXT – PORT JOUNIEH- ON THE PIER – JOE SITS BEHIND A TABLE, CHECKS THE US PASSPORTS AND THE RECOMMENDATIONS.

BA AND JIM WATCHING A GROUP OF TWENTY PASSENGERS BOARDING A YACHT AT THE PORT OF JOUNIEH.

        BA
Yes, Mr. Georges. Embassy personnel will meet you at Port Larnaca, and they will help and hint at you for your travel arrangements.
They know that you are on this yacht and will meet you there.
Have a nice trip!
Be aware of the Israelis in the middle of the sea. They might just check only your passports.

        GEORGES, PASSENGER
Je men fous, BA!
(I don't care.)
Je suis Americaine.
(I'm American.)
    (George, while laughing, indicates his US passport to BA)

        BA
    (Laughing)
Bon voyage, Georges.

FADE OUT:

FADE IN:

INT – BIG HALL – FIVE EMPLOYEES ARE SHARING TWO BIG TABLES. THERE IS A SMALL US FLAG ON ONE OF THE TABLES. A VISA MACHINE AND A SMALL SAFETY DEPOSIT BOX IS LOCATED ON ONE OF THE TABLES TOO.
JIM, LINDA, AND ONE EMPLOYEE INTERVIEW A CLIENT. BA IS AT THE ENTRANCE OF THE HALL, DISTRIBUTING AND EXPLAINING ITEMS ON THE FORMS.

SARKIS IS DISTRIBUTING NUMBERS TO THE CLIENTS WHO ARRIVE AND ARE SEATED OUTSIDE THE HALL.

INT – AT THE OTHER SIDE OF THE HALL, ANOTHER GROUP OF THREE EMPLOYEES SHARE A TABLE. A SMALL CANADIAN FLAG IS ON THE TABLE.

INT – A GROUP OF FOUR APPLICANTS APPROACH AND TALK TO BA WHILE HANDING HIM THEIR APPLICATION FORMS WITH LEBANESE PASSPORTS.

        BA
No, no. We can't issue tourist visas for the time being. These services are destined to US citizens only and very few emergency visitor visas.

        CLIENT
You don't issue tourist visas?

        BA
No, no! It's just very emergency cases.

        CLIENT
And what is that table with a Canadian flag there?

> BA

Oh, that group! Yes, our Canadian friends wanted to join us, and we share the room with them too.
They are also not issuing tourist visas.
They are here for only Canadian citizen services.

> CLIENT

When do you think is the embassy going to reopen?

> BA

We don't know!
In this period of Israeli and Syrian army occupation of Lebanon, we presume it will take longer than what we estimated.
Follow the local media!

INT – APPLICANT LEAVES THE LONG ROOM. BA APPROACHES LINDA AND CHATS WITH HER WHILE SITTING BESIDE HER AT THE NEXT AVAILABLE EMPTY CHAIR.

> BA

Linda, what are you doing up at the residence of the ambassador?

> LINDA

Nothing much, BA!
All the day, we are on the phones and answering some cables from the Department, etcetera.
It's boring.
I asked the ambassador to join you here and consult with you guys and see what we can do together.

> BA

Linda, now that we have a link to outside world, we can accept some applications and issue limited category visas.

LINDA
What do you mean with limited category visas?

BA
As you know, we have a lot of emergency medical cases: AUB professors, merchants, and some students.
We can handle them here.

LINDA
First, we need to consult the ambassador, and then we need a couple of employees to give us a hand, BA.
Can we handle all these applicants?

BA
Once you get the approval from the ambassador, I will contact my East Beirut employees, Linda.
We can use the manual system to issue visas and resume some of the consular work.
What do you say?

LINDA
Sounds Good to me!
Again, it depends from the ambassador's decision.

BA
Transfer my message to him, and don't worry for the management and administration of the workflow.
I will regulate and manage everything here.
Staying at home and doing nothing is really annoying.

LINDA
I understand!
Tonight, BA!
I will see him and transfer all our conversation to him and seek his advice and comments. And then I'll let you know tomorrow.

> BA
> Good girl!

> LINDA
> How is Marianno doing?

> BA
> In this situation, nothing.
> She is busy at home with the kids, and her rug shop is closed for the time being.
> You think Israeli and Syrian soldiers will buy Armenian rugs? They are in need of cheap whisky, cigarettes, and smuggled electrical equipment.

> LINDA
> You're right, BA.

INT - BA ENDS HIS CONVERSATION AND MOVES TOWARD JIM.

> BA
> Jim, it seems we're having two yachts per day instead of one.

> JIM
> Oh yes. It's a good sign that the link is operative and it's holding.

> BA
> Good. Everything is smooth except for some complaints from the citizens.
> Israelis are stopping every single yacht and searching to locate Palestinians onboard.

> JIM
> Oh my god!
> What are they going to do if they locate one?

>   Throw them to the sea?
>   We have citizens born in Palestine.
>
>   BA
>   They will interrogate!
>   Check if they carry Kalashnikov!
>   Ammunition!
>   And then negotiate together!
>   What do you say?
>
>   JIM
>   Israelis will eat them raw, BA!
>   Thank God. No one has yet been arrested.
>   Hope everything goes smoothly.

FADE OUT:

FADE IN:

INT – A BIG LONG HALL - JIM AND LINDA INTERVIEW APPLICANTS. TWO OTHER EMPLOYEES ARE SITTING BEHIND THE TABLE BESIDE THEM. THEY TRANSLATE, INTERVIEW, AND CHAT WITH APPLICANTS SITTING IN FRONT OF THE TABLES.

INT – BA IS HANDLING THE ARRIVAL OF NEW APPLICANTS AND CONTROLLING APPLICATIONS AND PASSPORTS.

INT – A SHORT THIN BEARDED OFFICER ENTERS THE ROOM. WIRELESS TELEPHONE BOX IN HIS HAND, HE SALUTES AND SHAKES HANDS WITH BA. HE APPROACHES JIM AND LINDA THEN ASKS BA TO JOIN HIM AT ONE OF THE CORNERS OF THE BIG HALL.

> BA
> Hi, Mr. Tom. Welcome to the new consulate!

> TOM
> Yes. Hi, BA.
> How are you?

> BA
> Good. For the time being, everything is okay.

> TOM
> Good! *Inshallah!*
> (With God's will.)

INT - TOM APPROACHES JIM AND LINDA, SALUTES WITH HIS HEAD, AND THEN CONTINUES HIS CONVERSATION.

> TOM
> Jim, Linda.
> How's it going?

> JIM
> Tom, as you see, recommendation after recommendation.

> LINDA
> Yeah, tourists to America! Some students and dozens of passport issuances!

INT – TOM, STILL STANDING IN FRONT OF THE DESKS, INDICATES A CORNER TO JIM AND LINDA.

> TOM
> BA, come join us.

> BA
> All right!

INT – TOM, JIM, LINDA, AND BA GATHER AT THE CORNER OF THE HALL AND CHAT.

> TOM
>
> Gentlemen, please listen carefully.
> I have a secret information to share with you guys.
> (Lights a cigarette)
> As of tomorrow, three pm GMT, we will have an order to evacuate our citizens from Port Jounieh.

> JIM
>
> We were expecting this, but not so soon!

> TOM
>
> The registration will begin tomorrow, seven AM local time, and continue up to three GMT.

> BA
>
> Do we have all the forms and the registration forms?

> TOM
>
> Be ready. Tomorrow morning, I will have all the formats ready for completion.

> LINDA
>
> Who's going to secure the land transportation?

> TOM
>
> Buses will be in front of the Municipality and carry our citizens and foreign-passport holders to the port.
> It's going to be a big one!
> Be prepared!
> BA, collect all your employees. We need them.
> (Looking at BA)
> You will be my personal assistant, and you will act as person-in-charge in my absence.

BA
Mr. Tom, I need some details.

TOM
Oh, I forgot!
One small suitcase per person. No excuses.
The foreign and local media will announce the decision as of six AM local time tomorrow.
We will accept the registration of other foreign nationals and evacuate them if and when we have availability.
BA, how many registered citizens do you think we have?

BA
I presume, whole Lebanon, around 2,500.
Divided between both sides (Christian and Muslim areas).

TOM
How many do you think will evacuate?

BA
What bothers me is West Beirut. If Muslims can cross to this side, all together, around 1,500.

TOM
Yeah! We estimated that.
All right then.
Be ready and see you in the morning.

FADE OUT:

FADE IN:

EXT – EARLY HOURS OF THE MORNING – THE SKY IS VIOLET, AND RED SPOTS BEHIND THE CLOUDS FROM THE SUN ARE OBVIOUS IN THE SKY. RADIO VOICE

Bedros Anserian

ANNOUNCEMENT IN THE BACKGROUND ANNOUNCES BREAKING NEWS IN ENGLISH.

"THIS IS THE BBC FROM LONDON. WE JUST LEARNED FROM OUR CORRESPONDENTS IN BEIRUT, LEBANON, THAT AS OF THIS MORNING, 3:00 GMT, THE US GOVERNMENT DECIDED TO EVACUATE ALL ITS CITIZENS FROM BEIRUT, LEBANON. NAVY UNITS OF THE US NAVY SIXTH FLEET AT THE MEDITERRANEAN WILL PARTICIPATE AND HELP IN THIS PROCEDURE TO EVACUATE ALL THE US CITIZENS IN LEBANON TO LEAVE THE COUNTRY. THE US AUTHORITIES URGES ITS CITIZENS TO CONTACT US EMBASSY PERSONNEL AT THE LOCAL MUNICIPALITY BUILDING, AT THE SEASHORE CITY OF JOUNIEH, TO FINALIZE THE EVACUATION PROCEDURES."

EXT – SUNNY DAY – EARLY HOURS OF THE MORNING - A HUGE CROWD OF PEOPLE FORMS IN FRONT OF THE MUNICIPALITY BUILDING OF JOUNIEH. TENS OF BUSES ARE ALSO PARKED IN FRONT OF THE BUILDING. ARMED VEHICLES WITH THE LEBANESE FORCES FLAGS PASS THE BUSY STREET IN FRONT OF THE BUILDING AND THE CROWD. PEOPLE—GATHERED GROUP BY GROUP IN FRONT OF THE MUNICIPALITY BUILDING—FOLLOW THE REGISTRATION PROCEDURES AT THE LOBBY OF THE BUILDING.

EXT – SUNNY DAY – EARLY HOURS OF THE MORNING - TWO DESKS ON THE RIGHT SIDE AND TWO DESKS ON THE LEFT SIDE OF THE MUNICIPALITY BUILDING ENTRANCE, WITH EMPLOYEES COMPLETING FORMS. TWO OFFICERS ARE EXPLAINING THE CONTENTS OF THE FORMS.
A LONG LINE OF CITIZENS, PASSPORTS IN THEIR HANDS, WAIT THEIR TURN FOR REGISTRATION.
ONE EMPLOYEE GIVES INSTRUCTIONS TO THE NEWLY ARRIVED EVACUEES.

> BA

Yes, ma'am. You are a citizen, and your husband can leave with you. Fill these two forms and bring them to this desk. Next!

> TOM

How's it going, BA?

> BA

As you see, Tom, we registered two hundred. And already, three buses left for the port area.
Also, I assigned three employees at the port area, and they will facilitate the exit registrations.

> TOM

Good job, BA!
Believe me, you will be rewarded for all these!

> BA

Oh! Okay, thank you.
By the way, we are registering other nationalities too.
Once we finalize our citizens, we will help them at the end.

> TOM

Oh yes. How many?
Did you count them?

> BA

Yes, Tom. Around thirty-five.

> TOM

Oh god.
Let them register, and we will manage to do something.
Push the citizens first, as much as you can.

                    LINDA
BA, can she take her sister with her?

                    BA
No, no, Linda. We are not authorized except the dependents: spouse, child, father, and mother only.

                    LINDA
                (Talking to evacuee)
See, I told you. He is in charge of this operation, but I tried to confirm.

FADE OUT:

FADE IN:

EXT – SUNNY AFTERNOON - PORT JOUNIEH
EIGHT LOCAL IMMIGRATION EMPLOYEES, WITH THEIR MILITARY DRESSES, SIT IN THE OPEN AIR AND, BEHIND TWO DESKS, CHECK THE PASSPORTS OF EVACUEES WHO ARE IN ONE LONG LINE.
THERE ARE THREE EMPLOYEES BEHIND THREE DESKS, AMERICAN FLAGS ON THE DESK BEYOND THE IMMIGRATION DESK ON THE PIER OF PORT JOUNIEH. THEY ARE NEAR THE US LANDING CRAFT, CHECKING FORMS AND PASSPORTS AND INSTRUCTING THE EVACUEES TO PROCEED TOWARD THE US VESSELS. AMERICAN FLAGS ARE ON THE CRAFT. FOUR MARINES GUARD THE CRAFT, AND FOUR MARINES ARE INSIDE THE CRAFT.
TWO MILITARY VEHICLES ARE ON PIER IN THE BACKGROUND, WITH LEBANESE FLAGS AND LEBANESE FORCES FLAGS MOUNTED ON THEM. THEY ARE GUARDING THE LOCATION.

BA
Tom, these are the last members. And we took also the whole foreign nationals as you said.

TOM
How many, total-total?

BA
Some 1,500 citizens and dependents and 56 foreign nationals, Tom.

TOM
I wish I can join them, BA!
What do you say?

BA
No, Tom. We don't let you this time.
We need you here, now.

TOM
I know! I know!
The ambassador will kill me if I leave!

BA
I didn't hear that, Tom.

TOM
You're right.
We are staying.

BA
The yacht didn't move today!

TOM
Of course. When we have a free safe ride to Larnaca, who needs the yacht ride?

>   BA
> Me and you, Tom!
>
>   BA AND TOM
> (Begin to laugh loudly)

EXT – SUNNY AFTERNOON – PORT JOUNIEH.
A GROUP OF EMPLOYEES APPROACH THE THREE DESKS MOUNTED WITH AMERICAN FLAGS AND WAVE TOWARD THE EVACUEES.
MARINES ARE HELPING THE LAST EVACUEES ENTER THE US LANDING CRAFT.
THE MARINE SERGEANT SALUTES TOM AND BA AND JUMPS INSIDE THE LANDING CRAFT.
THE LANDING CRAFT LEAVES SLOWLY.
THE EMPLOYEES ALL WAVE AT THE EVACUEES AND THE MARINES.
ON THE SEASIDE, IN THE BACKGROUND, THE LANDING CRAFT ADVANCES. IN THE MIDDLE OF THE HORIZON, IN THE MIST, THE US WARSHIP MANEUVERS INTO THE SEA.

>   BA
> Tom, Linda, Jim, come on. Let me invite you to a beer in our club! Let's celebrate!
>
>   JIM
> I will join, BA.
>
>   TOM
> Thanks, BA. I have to report about this operation to Mr. Ambassador. Take Linda with you too.

Diplomat, Without Portfolio

          LINDA
I wish I could, BA. Thanks anyhow. I have a lot to write and inform the Department at the residence. I have to go with Tom.
See you later!

EXT – LATE AFTERNOON SHADE - PIER OF PORT JOUNIEH EMPLOYEES CONGRATULATE EACH OTHER FOR THE EVACUATION WORK AND LEAVE IN VARIOUS GROUPS.

FADE OUT:

FADE IN:

INT – INSIDE A BAR – BA, IN BETWEEN JIM AND SARKIS, SITS ON THE BAR CHAIR. THE WALLS OF THE BAR ARE DECORATED WITH THE PAPER BILLS OF VARIOUS COUNTRIES WITH NOTES ON EACH BILL.
THE BARMAN IS SERVING CUSTOMERS AND PLACES SMALL PLATES OF PISTACHIOS AND CARROTS IN FRONT OF JIM, BA, AND SARKIS.

          JIM
BA, good job! We made it.
Have you any previous experience in evacuation procedures?

          BA
Once in 1976, I joined the embassy staff in preparation and registration!
At the same time, at the end, me and my wife were evacuated with the consular files to Piraeus, Athens.
We established the "Beirut Files" and resumed the consular work from our embassy in Athens.

                    JIM
That explains your professionalism, BA.
You were handling like an expert!
Congratulations. You deserve all the medals.

                    SARKIS
Of course. Today, we will drink until we become drunk!
          (Laughs)

                    BA
Yes. Let's drink for that, Jim.
          (BA raises the bottle of beer and touches Joe's and
          Sako's bottles in the air)

                    JIM
Right, BA. Let's drink for our success. And wait!

INT – JIM PULLS A FIVE-DOLLAR BILL FROM HIS POCKET AND ASKS BA AND SAKO TO SIGN ON THE BILL. JIM ADDS "SUCCESS THIS DAY" AND JUMPS FROM HIS BAR CHAIR AND CLIMBS ON A SEAT NEAR THE WALL. HE ATTACHES THE FIVE-DOLLAR BILL TO THE WALL WITH A PIN.

                    BA
Jim, you will return one day to Beirut.
We will come and visit this place and check if the bill exists here, the same place.

                    JIM
Definitely, BA!
I will come during peacetime.
I like this country.

                    SARKIS
Okay then. To our success and to your return one day!

FADE OUT:

FADE IN:

INT – NOONTIME – SOUNDS OF HEAVY SHOOTING OUTSIDE THE BUILDING

> LINDA, JIM, BA, KAMAL
> (All stand up, trying to get information from visitors)

> MUNICIPALITY SOLDIER
> (Crying and shouting, enters the room)
> They killed my president! My president!
> They killed President Bashir.

> LINDA, JIM
> (Stunned)
> What! What?
> President Bashir Gemayel was assassinated.

> BA
> Impossible.
> Oh my god. How?
> Where?

> LINDA
> This is unbelievable!
> We have to leave the office. We have to run. All of us!

THE WHOLE ROOM IS ASTONISHED AND STUNNED. THEY TRY TO GET INFORMATION FROM THE SOLDIER AND THE DIFFERENT EMPLOYEES OF THE BUILDING.

> JIM
> BA, this is a dangerous situation.

We have to dismiss the employees now.

          BA
Yes, Jim.
We have to! We can't stay here.
Let's move quickly and leave the hall.

EXT – NOONTIME –

LINDA, JIM, BA, AND THREE EMPLOYEES RUN TO THEIR CARS AND LEAVE THE BUILDING URGENTLY.

FADE OUT:

FADE IN:

INT - INSIDE A ROOM – TV SET

ANNOUNCEMENT – THE CHRISTIAN MILITIAS, ALONG WITH ISRAELI SOLDIERS, ATTACK THE SABRA AND SHATILA PALESTINIAN CAMPS. HUNDREDS OF CASUALTIES, WHICH INCLUDES WOMEN AND CHILDREN.

          BA
          (Frozen and disturbed by the news)
A new war page just opened.
Who was thinking about these developments?
Mariano, can't believe my ears and eyes.
We will open a new page of war in Lebanon.

          MARIANO
God save us! Amen.

FADE OUT:

Diplomat, Without Portfolio

FADE IN:

INT – NOONTIME – INSIDE A WELL-DECORATED ROOM AT THE CONSULAR SECTION, AMERICAN EMBASSY.
A MEETING BETWEEN DENIS, CONS GEN, LINDA, AND BA.
CONS GEN HOLDING NOTES AND LINDA AND BA RECORDING SOME DETAILS ON THEIR NOTEBOOKS.

    DENIS
    (Looks relaxed but worried)
BA, now that the Israelis have withdrawn and the multinational forces are in the country, we expect additional workload of applicants.
We have to manage the reception with additional employees.

    BA
    (Shows readiness to implement the system)
I will do that and add two more employees on the counters.

    LINDA
    (Very relaxed and ready to work)
Shall we begin to issue the full five years validity visas or not yet?

    DENIS
    (Indicating with her finger)
Yes. BA was there during our meeting. He heard what I said to the minister of foreign affairs.
We promised and advised the minister that we will implement the full validity immediately, on condition that the Lebanese will not request visas of officers, admitted as members of multinational forces at the port of entry, Beirut International Airport.
So we have to begin with that immediately.

> LINDA
> (Showing readiness)

All right!
Let's jump.
We have a huge queue already outside the consulate.

> BA
> (Suggesting)

Linda, we have to limit the number of the applicants!
We can't handle more than six hundred cases per day.
Just check the queue. It reached up to the main entrance of the embassy.

> DENIS

Right! We can't handle more than six hundred cases per day. BA, instruct the reception desk to stop distributing numbers once they reach six hundred.

> BA
> (Jumps from his seat)

Okay, done.

FADE OUT:

FADE IN:

INT – CAFÉ IN JOUNIEH – TWO PEOPLE ARE SEATED ON THE BAR AND DRINKING BEER.

BA AND JIM DISCUSSING, WIPING TEARS, AND TALKING.

> BA

I told you. I left one more surprise location to bring you today. Remember how we spent our nights here after office hours at the Municipality?

> JIM

Even Mr. Ambassador wished he could join us to have a cold beer!

> BARMAN ELIE

BA, Joe, this one is on the house!
Two old friends, our guests after thirty years.
Memories. We will never forget you.

> JIM

With your permission, Elie, I will check if our US five-dollar bill still exists on the wall.

> BARMAN ELIE

Yes, why not! Check it, Jim.

(Jim jumps from his bar chair and goes to the corner of the bar. He gets an empty chair and climbs on it. He tries to locate the five-dollar bill on the wall, which is covered with various paper currencies.)

> JIM
> (Indicates with his finger)

I found it!
BA, Elie, just found it. It's here.
Oh gosh. What a surprise. After thirty years!

> BARMAN ELIE

I told you. It remains here as long as we are here and reminds us of your presence, Jim.

> JIM

I don't believe it!
Tears in my eyes, Elie.
This is for you and your bar and all your staff!
Thank you.
> (Jim drinks the whole glass)

(Elie, the barman, pours new beer into the glasses of BA, Sam, and Jim. Tears in his eyes and excited.)

> BA
> Unforgettable, Good memories, Elie. You were…we were younger, friends. Elie, you remember how we managed to evacuate through the embassy your whole TMA crew from here to Larnaca?

> ELIE/BARMAN
> What a week! What a day it was! With your help, we went back to operate. Thank you, guys! Good Guys.

(Elie drinks the whole contents of the glass.)

CUT TO:

FADE IN:

EXT – SEASIDE CORNICHE, NICE BEAUTIFUL BLUE SKY.

BA DRIVES A BMW CAR WHILE JIM, SITTING ON THE PASSENGER SEAT, WATCHES THE SEASIDE RESTAURANTS AND CAFÉS. THERE IS A MOSQUE ON THE BACKGROUND, FACING THE HARD ROCK CAFÉ.

BA POINTS OUT THE HIGH-RISE BUILDINGS AND HOTELS ON THE SEASIDE.

> BA
> During your service, this area was devastated and deserted. I'm sure you were not authorized to walk in this area. See how it is developed in a short period of time.

> JIM
> Oh, BA. This is fantastic. Nice architecture and modern buildings.
> Amazing.

> BA
> This is where PM Hariri was assassinated!
> Destruction was huge and costly, with human beings shattered all over.
> But this is Beirut!
> A mixture of war and peace.
> Ugly and beautiful.
> Devil and angel.
> Translate as you wish.

FADE OUT:

EXT. CORNISH RUE THE FRANCE - DAY

Seaside view, beautiful blue sky opposite a modern new building. BA and Jim discuss and search together, while Sam is beside them, a location on a map and a couple of photos.

> BA
> (Indicates a building)
> I told you, the building does not exist anymore!

> JIM
> (Looking toward the building)
> Oh my god, what happened here? It looks like a Modern city and a modern corner. Where is the building?

> **BA**
> They told me that the landlord sold the land to a Gulf investor. Then it was planned to construct an office building here.

Jim looking at the building and toward the sea.

> **JIM**
> I remember my office had to be on the fourth floor overlooking the sea. It was quite a nice view.
> Alas! I can't see my office now.

BA indicating a location on the building.

> **BA**
> Those were the days Jim! My office was on the first floor and I had a nice sea view too. They are all gone now. Memories.

> **JIM**
> So this was our building… (Pulls a photo from BA's hand.) Sam, this location supposedly…was my office…and now they built this nice building with an entrance on the south side of the building…

Jim tries to figure out the entrance of the building.

> **JIM (CONT'D)**
> Instead of the middle of the building. And the snack bar was located here…street level. If I had gone for lunch the day of the bombing, I would surely have been killed because when the bomb detonated, propane tanks in the kitchen exploded, killing all but one person in the snack bar. That was Anne. (Pauses and thinks.) There is conclusive evidence that through Hezbollah, the Iranian security service funded and directed the whole operation… Imad Moughnieh was the mastermind, behind all these tragedies, backed by Iran.

In the end, he was killed by a car bomb by his employers, friends in Damascus, to hide his activities against US and internationally… BA, do you know if they found any bodies buried underneath?

BA
(Frozen in his location)
They said they located human remains and parts they sent them to the AUH morgue. Poor guys… "They came in peace…"
The very presence of the embassy in the midst of the war in Lebanon was an assertion of hope that Lebanon would soon return to normal life. (Pause.) Unfortunately, many more years were to pass before Lebanon could achieve a degree of stability.

JIM
After the 1983 embassy attack, the Department of State imposed new security standards on Embassies around the world. The security measures may have made our embassies and consulates safer, but it is impossible to conduct diplomacy from a bunker.

BA
(Stunned)
The bombing taught Americans that peaceful intentions were not enough to protect us from those who would use terror to achieve their goals in the Middle East. It taught us the stakes of involvement in this region. Yes, first you have to understand the culture, traditions, and habits. You have to respect their religion and speak their language, study their geography and history and accordingly defend yourself. (Pause.) Jim, I have my last question for you! Why does a US diplomat want to accept a new assignment like Beirut?

> JIM
> (Eyes opened widely)
> This is where the challenge is! This is where we can make a difference. Diplomacy has become a risky business, and our diplomats know this. In a bunker, it is also difficult to have the rewarding and productive interaction with local colleagues that I enjoyed with my Lebanese staff. (Tears in his eyes.) With this beautiful scene and beautiful weather, I can't stand it anymore B A.

Jim, BA, and Sam freeze for a while.

> JIM (CONT'D)
> Come on, guys! Let's leave this area. I can't handle it anymore. It was supposed to be our…graveyard, instead.

Indicating the building behind.

> Cowards! Let's leave… (Jim pauses.)
> Thank you, BA, thank you for bringing me here. (Returns toward the building.) Rest in peace, my friends. (Begins to cry.)

> BA
> (Hugs Jim while crying)
> They are with us always, Jim. We will never forget them.

CUT TO:

EXT. BEIRUT HARIRI INTERNATIONAL AIRPORT - DAY

Departure section of Beirut Hariri International Airport - Sunny day

> BA
> (Hugs Jim)
> Thank you for coming, Jim. We were relieved and remembered our old days in Beirut.
>
> JIM
> BA, my friend, thank you for everything. Without you, our stay would have no meaning in Beirut. Me and Sam appreciate what you have done. See you in the States!
>
> SAM
> (Hugs BA)
> Thank you, BA, for everything.

Jim and Sam enter the departure section of the airport.

CUT TO:

EXT. BEIRUT CORNISH, SEASIDE - DAY

BA sitting on the bench, seaside Beirut Cornish, facing the sea. OS background Italian song by Joe Divierro, "Adieu Beirut."

Quick scenes from new Beirut with background music by Joe Divierro.

FADE OUT:

THE END

NARRATIVES ON THE SCREEN SCROLLS

- October 23, 1983 - Just twelve days after Ambassador Dillon left Lebanon, a suicide bomber attacked the US Marine Barracks at Beirut Airport, killing 241 American Servicemen.

Bedros Anserian

- January 18, 1984 - AUB president Malcolm Kerr was murdered outside his office.

- March 16, 1984 - William Buckley, CIA station chief in Beirut, was kidnapped outside his apartment. In October, Hezbollah distributed a photo of Buckley's corpse.

- September 20, 1984 - The American Embassy, now relocated to East Beirut for greater security, was attacked and 22 people were killed.

- May 8, 2006 - BA and his family members left Beirut and immigrated to Los Angeles, California. In Los Angeles, BA joined a professional law firm and still works as a legal assistant and immigration specialist.

They Came In Peace

June 16, 1976

- Ambassador Francis E. Meloy
- Zouhier M. Mograbi
- Robert 0. Waring

April 18, 1983 - US Embassy

- Riad Abdul Massih
- Abdallah Al-Halabi
- Yolla Al-Hashim
- Hassan Ali Yehya
- Robert Ames
- Mohamedain Assaran
- Elias Atallah
- Cesar Bathiard
- Thomas Blacka
- Antoine Daccache

- Mounir Dandan
- Rafic Eid
- Naja El-Kaddoum
- Farouk Fanous
- Phyliss Faraci
- Terry-Lee Gilden
- Kenneth Haas
- Hussein Haidar-Ahmad
- Mohamed Hasssan
- Deborah Hixon
- Mohamed Ibrahim
- Raja Iskandarani
- Frank Johnston
- Nazih Juraydini
- Ghazi Kabbout
- Antoine Karam
- Raymond Karkour
- Edgard Khuri
- Hafez Khuri
- James Lewis
- Monique Lewis
- Amal Ma'akaroun
- SSGT Ben H. Maxwell, USA
- William McIntyre
- CPL Robert V. McMaugh, USMC
- Mary Metni
- Kamal Nahhas
- Jirjis Naja
- Antoine Najem
- Nabih Rahhal
- Darwish Ra'i
- Roudayna Sahyoun
- Fouad Salameh
- SSGT Mark E. Salazar, USA
- Suad Sarrouh
- Shahe Setrakian

- William Sheil
- Nabih Shoubeir
- Janet Stevens
- SFC Richard Twine, USA
- Albert Votaw
- Khalil Yatim

August 29, 1983

- 2NDLT Donald G. Losey, USMC
- SSGT Alexander M. Ortega, USMC

SEPTEMBER 6, 1983

- LCPL Randy W. Clark, USMC
- CPL Pedro J. Valle, USMC

OCTOBER 14, 1983

- SGT Alan H. Soifert, USMC

OCTOBER 16, 1983

- CAPT Michael J. Ohler, USMC

October 23, 1983 - **US Marine Corps Barracks**

- CPL Terry W. Abbott, USMC
- LCPL Clemon S. Alexander, USMC
- PFC John R. Allman, USMC
- CPL Moses J. Arnold JR., USMC
- PFC Charles K. B Ailey, USMC
- LCPL Nicholas B Aker, USMC
- LCPL Johnsen B Anks, USMC
- LCPL Richard E. B Arrett, USMC
- HM1 Ronny K. B Ates, USN

Diplomat, Without Portfolio

- 1STSGT David L. B Attle, USMC
- LCPL James R. B Aynard, USMC
- HN Jesse W. Beamon, USN
- GYSGT Alvin Belmer, USMC
- PFC Stephen Bland, USMC
- SGT Richard L. Blankenship, USMC
- LCPL John W. Blocker, USMC
- CAPT Joseph J. Boccia JR., USMC
- CPL Leon Bohannon JR., USMC
- SSGT John R. Bohnet JR., USMC
- CPL John J. Bonk JR., USMC
- LCPL Jeffrey L. Boulos, USMC
- CPL David R. Bousum, USMC
- 1STLT John N. Boyett, USMC
- CPL Anthony Brown, USMC
- LCPL David W. Brown, USMC
- LCPL Bobby S. Buchanan JR., USMC
- CPL John B. Buckmaster, USMC
- PFC William F. Burley, USMC
- HN Jimmy R. Cain, USN
- CPL Paul L. Callahan, USMC
- SGT Mecot E. Camara, USMC
- PFC Bradly J. Campus, USMC
- LCPL Johnnie D. Ceasar, USMC
- PFC Marc L. Cole, USMC
- SP4 Marcus A. Coleman, USA
- PFC Juan M. Comas, USMC
- SGT Robert A. Conley, USMC
- CPL Charles D. Cook, USMC
- LCPL Curtis J. Cooper, USMC
- LCPL Johnny L. Copeland, USMC
- CPL Bert D. Corcoran, USMC
- LCPL David L. Cosner, USMC
- SGT Kevin P. Coulman, USMC
- LCPL Brett A. Croft, USMC
- LCPL Rick R. Crudale, USMC

- LCPL Kevin P. Custard, USMC
- LCPL Russell E. Cyzick, USMC
- MAJ Andrew L. Davis, USMC
- PFC Sidney S. Decker, USMC
- PFC Michael J. Devlin, USMC
- LCPL Thomas A. Dibenedetto, USMC
- PVT Nathaniel G. Dorsey, USMC
- SGTMAJ Frederick B. Douglass, USMC
- CPL Timothy J. Dunnigan, USMC
- HN Bryan L. Earle, USN
- MSGT Roy L. Edwards, USMC
- HM3 William D. Elliot JR., USN
- LCPL Jesse Ellison, USMC
- PFC Danny R. Estes, USMC
- PFC Sean F. Estler, USMC
- HM3 James E. Faulk, USN
- PFC Richard A. Fluegel, USMC
- CPL Steven M. Forrester, USMC
- HM3 William B. Foster JR., USN
- CPL Michael D. Fulcher, USMC
- LCPL Benjamin E. Fuller, USMC
- LCPL Michael S. Fulton, USMC
- CPL William Gaines JR., USMC
- LCPL Sean R. Gallagher, USMC
- LCPL David B. Gander, USMC
- LCPL George M. Gangur, USMC
- SSGT Leland E. Gann, USMC
- LCPL Randall J. Garcia, USMC
- SSGT Ronald J. Garcia, USMC
- LCPL David D. Gay, USMC
- SSGT Harold D. Ghumm, USMC
- LCPL Warner Gibbs JR., USMC
- CPL Timothy R. Giblin, USMC
- ETC Michael W. Gorchinski, USN
- LCPL Richard J. Gordon, USMC
- LCPL Harold F. Gratton, USMC

Diplomat, Without Portfolio

- SGT Robert B. Greaser, USMC
- LCPL Davin M. Green, USMC
- LCPL Thomas A. Hairston, USMC
- SGT Freddie Haltiwanger JR., USMC
- LCPL Virgil D. Hamilton, USMC
- SGT Gilbert Hanton, USMC
- LCPL William Hart, USMC
- CAPT Michael S. Haskell, USMC
- PFC Michael A. Hastings, USMC
- CAPT Paul A. Hein, USMC
- LCPL Douglas E. held, USMC
- PFC Mark A. Helms, USMC
- LCPL Ferrandy D. Henderson, USMC
- SSGT John Hendrickson, USMC
- MSGT Matilde Hernandez JR., USMC
- CPL Stanley G. Hester, USMC
- GYSGT Donald W. Hildreth, USMC
- SSGT Richard H. Holberton, USMC
- HM3 Robert S. Holland, USN
- LCPL Bruce A Hollingshead, USMC
- PFC Melvin D. Holmes, USMC
- CPL Bruce L. Howard, USMC
- LT John R Hudson, USN
- CPL Terry L. Hudson, USMC
- LCPL Lyndon J. Hue, USMC
- 2NDLT Maurice E. Hukill, USMC
- LCPL Edward F. Iacovino JR, USMC
- PFC John J. Ingalls, USMC
- W01 Paul G. Innocenzi III, USMC
- LCPL James J. Jackowski, USMC
- LCPL Jeffrey W. James, USMC
- LCPL Nathaniel W. Jenkins, USMC
- HM2 Michael H. Johnson, USN
- CPL Edward A Johnston, USMC
- LCPL Steven Jones, USMC
- PFC Thomas A Julian, USMC

- HM2 Marion E. Kees, USN
- SGT Thomas C. Keown, USMC
- GYSGT Edward E. Kimm, USMC
- LCPL Walter V Kingsley, USMC
- SGT Daniel S. Kluck, USA
- LCPL James C. Knipple, USMC
- LCPL Freas H. Kreischer III, USMC
- LCPL Keith J. Laise, USMC
- LCPL Thomas G. Lamb, USMC
- LCPL James J. Langon IV, USMC
- SGT Michael S. Lariviere, USMC
- CPL Steven B. Lariviere, USMC
- MSGT Richard L. Lemnah, USMC
- CPL David A. Lewis, USMC
- SGT Val S. Lewis, USMC
- CPL Joseph R. Livingston, USMC
- LCPL Paul D. Lyon JR., USMC
- MAJ John W. Macroglou, USMC
- CPL Samuel Maitland, USMC
- SSGT Charlie R. Martin, USMC
- PFC Jack L. Martin, USMC
- CPL David S. Massa, USMC
- SGT Michael R. Massman, USMC
- PVT Joseph J. Mattacchione, USMC
- LCPL John McCall, USMC
- SGT James E. McDonough, USMC
- LCPL Timothy R. McMahon, USMC
- LCPL Timothy D. McNeely, USMC
- HM2 George N. McVicker II, USN
- PFC Louis Melendez, USMC
- SGT Richard H. Menkins II, USMC
- CPL Michael D. Mercer, USMC
- LCPL Ronald W. Meurer, USMC
- HM3 Joseph P. Milano, USN
- CPL Joseph P. Moore, USMC
- LCPL Richard A. Morrow, USMC

Diplomat, Without Portfolio

- LCPL John F. Muffler, USMC
- CPL Alex Munoz, USMC
- CPL Harry D. Myers, USMC
- 1STLT David J. Nairn, USMC
- LCPL Luis A. Nava, USMC
- CPL John A. Olson, USMC
- PFC Robert P. Olson, USMC
- CWO3 Richard C. Ortiz, USMC
- PFC Jeffrey B. Owen, USMC
- CPL Joseph A. Owens, USMC
- CPL Connie Ray Page, USMC
- LCPL Ulysses Parker, USMC
- LCPL Mark W. Payne, USMC
- GYSGT John L. Pearson, USMC
- PFC Thomas S. Perron, USMC
- SGT John A. Phillips JR., USMC
- HMC George W. Piercy, USN
- 1STLT Clyde W. Plymel, USMC
- SGT William H. Pollard, USMC
- SGT Rafael I. Pomalestorres, USMC
- CPL Victor M. Prevatt, USMC
- PFC James C. Price, USMC
- SSGT Patrick K. Prindeville, USMC
- PFC Eric A. Pulliam, USMC
- HM3 Diomedes J. Quirante, USN
- LCPL David M. Randolph, USMC
- GYSGT Charles R. Ray, USMC
- PFC Rui A. Relvas, USMC
- PFC Terrance L. Rich, USMC
- LCPL Warren Richardson, USMC
- SGT Juan C. Rodriguez, USMC
- LCPL Louis J. Rotondo, USMC
- LCPL Guillermo Sanpedro JR., USMC
- LCPL Michael C. Sauls, USMC
- 1STLT Charles J. Schnorf, USMC
- PFC Scott L. Schultz, USMC

- CAPT Peter J. ScialabB A, USMC
- CPL Gary R. Scott, USMC
- CPL Ronald L. Shalla, USMC
- CPL Thomas A. Shipp, USMC
- LCPL Jerry! D. Shropshire, USMC
- LCPL James F. Silvia, USMC
- LCPL Larry H. Simpson JR., USMC
- LCPL Stanley J. Sliwinski, USMC
- LCPL Kirk H. Smith, USMC
- SSGT Thomas G. Smith, USMC
- CAPT Vincent L. Smith, USMC
- LCPL Edward Soares, USMC
- 1STLT William S. Sommerhof, USMC
- LCPL Michael C. Spaulding, USMC
- LCPL John W. Spearing, USMC
- LCPL Stephen E. Spencer, USMC
- LCPL Bill J. Stelpflug, USMC
- LCPL Horace R. Stephens, USMC
- PFC Craig S. Stockton, USMC
- LCPL Jeffrey G. Stokes, USMC
- LCPL Thomas D. Stowe, USMC
- LCPL Eric D. Sturghill, USMC
- LCPL Devon L. Sundar, USMC
- LT James F. Surch JR., USN
- CPL Dennis A. Thompson, USMC
- SSGT Thomas P. Thorstad, USMC
- PFC Stephen D. Tingley, USMC
- LCPL John J. Tishmack, USMC PFC
- Donald H. Vallone JR., USMC
- CPL Eric R. Walker, USMC
- CPL Leonard W. Walker, USMC
- CPL Eric G. Washington, USMC
- CPL Obrian Weekes, USMC
- 1STSGT Tandy W. Wells, USMC
- LCPL Steven B. Wentworth, USMC
- SGT Allen D. Wesley, USMC

Diplomat, Without Portfolio

- GYSGT Lloyd D. West, USMC
- SSGT John R. Weyl, USMC
- CPL Burton D. Wherland JR., USMC
- LCPL Dwayne W. Wigglesworth, USMC
- LCPL Rodney J. Williams, USMC
- GYSGT Scipio Williams JR., USMC
- LCPL Johnny A. Williamson, USMC
- CAPT Walter E. Wint JR., USMC
- CAPT William E. Winter, USMC
- CPL John E. Wolfe, USMC
- 1STLT Donald E. Woollett, USMC
- HM3 David E. Worley, USN
- PFC Craig L. Wyche, USMC
- SFC James G. Yarber, USA
- SGT Jeffrey D. Young, USMC
- 1STLT William A. Zimmerman

December 2, 1983

- CPL Henry Townsend JR., USMC

December 4, 1983

- CPL Shannon D. Biddle, USMC
- CPL Sam Gherman, USMC
- SGT Manuel A. Cox, USMC
- CPL David L. Daugherty, USMC
- CPL Thomas A. Evans, USMC
- PFC Jeffrey T. Hattaway, USMC
- CPL Todd A. Kraft, USMC
- LT Mark A. Lange, USN
- CPL Marvin H. Perkins, USMC

January 8, 1984

- CPL Edward J. Gargano, USMC

Bedros Anserian

January 30, 1984

- LCPL George L. Dramis, USMC
- LCPL Rodolfo Hernandez, USMC

February 9, 1984

- CPT Alfred Butler Ill, USMC

October 20, 1984

- CPL Michael Hasenfus, USA

September 20, 1984 - **US Embassy Annex**

- Fouad Abdou
- Kassem Ayache
- Edward Maalouf
- Walid Minkara
- Jad Nasr
- Nelly Saoud
- Ali-Fayez Tayyar
- IS1 Michael R. Wagner, USN
- W02 Kenneth V. Welch, USA

Diplomat, Without Portfolio

7 floor embassy collapsed

10 Year service award with ambassador Dillon and DCM Pugh In Beirut

At the Main Entrance of the American Embassy Beirut
two months before the bombing of the American Embassy.
Meritorius Honor Award to embassy Personnel

Diplomat, Without Portfolio

Bedros Anserian - Supervisor Visa Section Beirut, Lebanon

Bedros Anserian - Toddler

Diplomat, Without Portfolio

Bedros Anserian Decorating Rotary Pin to David M, Sutherfield, Acting Ast. Sec Bureau of N.E. Affairs

Bedros Anserian with Ambassador Edward Jerejian

Bedros Anserian with Father and Mother

Diplomat, Without Portfolio

Bedros being carried out of the bombed Embassy in Beirut, Lebanon

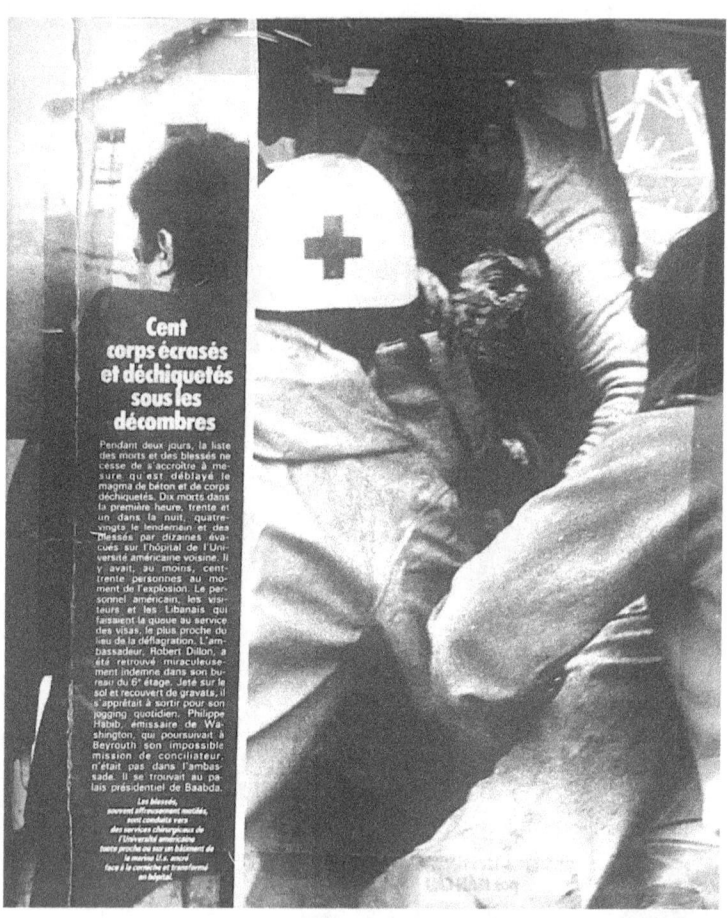

Bedros Anserian

Bedros being carried out to Ambulance courtesy of parismatch

Diplomat, Without Portfolio

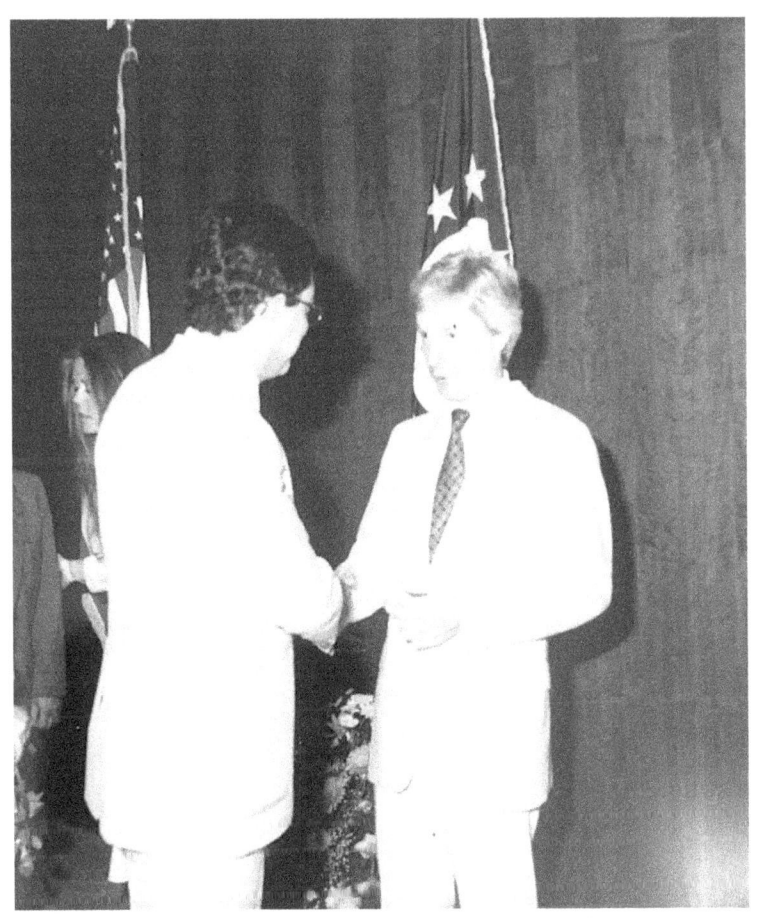

Bedros with Ambassador Ryan David Crocker in Beirut July 4th, 1990

Bedros with John Reed, Seta Ourfalian Nahas and Leo Pezzi at the balcony of the Department of State

Gathering with Former Consgen Richard Williams, Cons Rebecca J. McCullough, Margaret Murphy and Consular Employees

Diplomat, Without Portfolio

25th anniversary celebration at main entrance of the Department of State with family members of the victims & survivors and injured employees.

The Two Survivors Bedros Anserian and Mary Apovian Infront of Memorial Park at the anex of The American Embassy in Beirut

Bedros Anserian

Bedros Anserian with Senator Robert Menendez, at 75th Anniversary of Tekeyan Cultural Association banquet

Diplomat, Without Portfolio

Bedros and Marianne Anserians

"We have done our best to avoid mistakes. And if mistakes are found, we seek the reader's understanding and his/her forgiveness."

ABOUT THE AUTHOR

Bedros Hagop Anserian (A.k.a. Anserlian)

Bedros Anserlian—born in Beirut, grandson of Bedros, son of Hagop and Lousine Iskenian—is married to Marianne Hovagim Tatevossian. They have two children: Hagop (NDU system engineer) and Alexandra Klavdia (NDU business computing).

He graduated from AGBU / Hovagimian-Manougian Sec. School and continued his higher education in various institutes with AUB in Lebanon (specializing in business administration) and with Kaplan University in the US (as a paralegal). He attended various consular seminars at the Foreign Service Institute at the Department of State in Washington, DC.

After graduation, he joined the Nazarian establishment as an accountant and then moved to a foreign diplomatic mission. He had worked in the American embassies in Beirut, Athens, Cairo, Nicosia, and Sanaa for eighteen years. As a chief of the consular section in

Athens, Greece, he acted as a liaison officer between the American embassies of Athens and Beirut.

He was awarded with many certificates of achievements (from Richard Murphy, Cyrus Vance, etc.).

He was one of the survivors of the bombing of the American embassy in Beirut in April 1983.

In 1987, for his dedication and continuous devotion and duty, he was nominated for the Best Foreign Service National Employee of the Year at the American embassy in Athens, Greece.

He volunteered as an honorary secretary of AGBU-AYA Knights Asbedner from 1989 to 1998 in Beirut. He was the chairman of the Aintab Compatriot Union, Beirut chapter, from 1991 to 1992 and board member up to 2006. He was nominated by the president of Armenia, Levon Ter-Petrosyan, as a board member of the Hymnatram Beirut chapter for Relief to Armenia from 1994 to 1996. He is a Rotarian and founding vice president and past president of Sahel Metn Club of Lebanon. During his presidency from 1999 to 2000, as a major project of the club, the new roundabout of Bourj Hammoud, Lebanon, has been reconstructed and renovated.

Between 1989 and 2005, along with his brother Nerces and sister Amive, he established a travel agency in Beirut known as Anser Travel. As a team member of the Lebanese official delegation (along with Lebanese minister of transportation Mr. Omar Meskawi and former minister and deputy Mr. Souren Khanamirlan) in October 1993, participated in Yerevan with the negotiations in the reopening of the air link between Yerevan and Beirut.

Between 1993 and 2001, Anser Travel represented in Beirut, the newly established Armenian Airlines and, later, the Armenian International Airways. Besides the sales of tickets, they organized regular tours to Armenia and Artzakh (Nagomi Gharapagh).

For years, his articles about travel and tourism appeared in the *TIDAG*, an Armenian monthly magazine in Beirut. He is the author of the published movie script "Diplomat Without Portfolio" and his book, *Anserlian Dynasty*, which was released in April 2023.

Between 2006 and 2016, in Los Angeles, he was employed as a legal assistant / immigration specialist with the Karlin & Karlin Professional Law Corporation.

Since 2010, he has been an active parish council member of the Western Diocese of the Armenian Church. He chairs the parish council, and at the same time, he is a diocesan council member.